Reparation
A Julian Mercer Thriller

G.K. Parks

Copyright © 2018 G.K. Parks

A Modus Operandi imprint

ISBN:
ISBN-13: 978-1-942710-12-7

For my mom and dad

ONE

Julian Mercer pushed away from the computer screen and stared out the window. It was raining, as usual. No wonder it was always so bloody foggy in London. He took a deep breath and stretched his arms over his head, hearing an unsettling crunch resonating from his shoulder. The old injury never healed properly. More accurately, he never gave it time to heal. It might have also helped if an actual doctor reset the dislocation instead of his teammate, but that was neither here nor there. Time was something the K&R specialists often lacked. So having months and months of nothing but time at home was driving Mercer batty.

Crossing to the bar, he filled a glass with scotch and took a sip. Drinking was one way to pass these insipid days and nights. It's not like he could tell the difference when there was nothing but gloom. He snorted at the ludicrous thought. He was projecting his emotional state on the world.

"Cheers." He held the glass up to his reflection. His

reflection nodded sagely and drank.

"Jules, who are you talking to?" Bastian Clarke stumbled into the living room of their rented flat, eyeing the drink curiously. "Have you been up all night?"

"It's morning?" Mercer asked. A simple fact he failed to notice.

Bastian let out a sigh and continued into the kitchen. "It's seven. On a Tuesday." After setting the coffee to brew, he returned to the living room. "Is that whiskey?"

"Scotch whiskey."

"Did I mention it's seven a.m.? Oh seven hundred? Sound familiar?"

Mercer emptied the glass in one big swallow, ignoring the burn at the back of his throat. He went to the bar and selected a different bottle. "Shall I make your coffee Irish?"

"No, mate. One of us needs to be productive today." He slid behind the computer. "Any luck on the surveillance footage?"

Mercer sighed, his gaze returning to the window.

"I take it that's why we're day drinking." Bastian clicked a few keys. "Alexis Parker compiled a list of vehicles. I ran the plates. Do you want to take a look at the names and see if any of them ring a bell?"

"I already did. They don't." Steeling his emotions, Mercer turned back around to face his second-in-command. "Stop pretending. We know whoever killed Michelle wasn't caught on a surveillance camera." Just saying his wife's name felt like a punch to the gut. For a moment, he could see nothing but the sight of her on their kitchen floor. Blood pooled around her, and she gasped. He held her, promised her things he knew he couldn't give, and begged to trade his life for hers. In the end, none of it mattered. She was gone, and he was broken and alone. "Do you think he altered the footage or looped the feed?"

"It's a possibility." Hearing the beep of the coffeemaker, Bastian went into the kitchen and filled a mug. "The footage doesn't show any obvious signs of tampering, but I'll check it again. You should get some sleep."

Mercer found the notion laughable. He couldn't remember the last time he slept soundly since being sequestered in London. The closest he'd come to a good night's rest was blacking out after one too many drinks, and even that didn't keep the nightmares at bay.

"In a bit. I'm going to check on Hans. He's supposed to be released from the hospital tomorrow. I'll see if he needs anything."

"The doctors are hopeful that's the last of his surgeries. His mum has his room all ready."

"I'll arrange whatever home care he needs. Nurses, physical therapists, whatever."

"Knowing Hans, he probably has every bird in the hospital catering to his every whim. The security specialist who nearly had his arm lobbed off while saving a young lad. It's a good story."

"Aside from the machete separating his shoulder from his body," Mercer retorted.

"Aye, mate. Except for that."

Mercer clipped his holster to his belt at the small of his back and shrugged into a jacket. He considered taking one of their vehicles but decided not to risk it. Drinking and driving wasn't recommended, particularly when the coppers had it out for him. He didn't need to give them any additional reasons to detain him. Perhaps, he'd detour before returning and visit that arsehole inspector who failed to conduct a proper investigation, thus allowing his wife's killer to roam freely. If that self-righteous investigator had a few functioning brain cells, he would have realized immediately Mercer wasn't the killer and continued to explore leads, instead of blaming the husband and letting the case grow cold.

"Bastard."

Bastian gave him a curious look. "What was that?"

Shaking his head, Mercer went to the door. "I'll be back later."

"You sure you're okay?"

Not bothering to supply an answer, Mercer stepped into the frigid rain, pulling the door closed behind him. The hair prickled at the back of his neck. Ignoring the gnawing in his gut, he chose to believe it was the lousy, cold weather causing the twitchy unease. But in truth, he felt it almost every time he ventured out. Something wasn't right.

After being in Her Majesty's service for years as a commander in the Special Air Service, Mercer wasn't equipped to remain stationary. Being in one place too long led to carelessness. It gave the enemy time to discover one's position and plan a surprise attack. But when Mercer spoke to Bastian about it, the analyst shrugged it off as nothing but paranoia. It was no secret Mercer despised London. He had plenty of reasons, but what he felt as he walked the streets wasn't due to grief or guilt. Someone was out there, watching. He could feel it.

As usual, he selected a different route to the hospital. After crossing a few streets and heading in the opposite direction, he paused beneath the covered awning of a bus stop. He scanned the area but didn't spot anyone suspicious. Several commuters were waiting. He stood off to the side, watching with intense focus. When the bus came, he moved through the crowd, getting lost among the passengers disembarking and those climbing on board. A few blocks later, he caught a cab.

While the driver dithered on about one of the football clubs, Mercer watched for a possible tail. With the dense city traffic and the way the driver wove in and out of the lanes, it was nearly impossible to tell if anyone was following them, but when the cab stopped at its destination, no familiar vehicles were in sight. Mercer paid and stepped out, his senses on high alert.

By the time he made it to Hans Bauer's room, the prickly sensation was gone. He knocked gently against the doorjamb. As predicted, the reconnaissance expert was back to his roguish ways. Presently, he was being spoon-fed by a leggy nursing assistant.

Mercer strode into the room, nodding at the woman who blushed a bright scarlet. She dabbed Hans' mouth with the napkin, gave him a peck on the cheek, and smiled uncomfortably as she scurried past.

Hans pushed the tray table away with his good arm and sat up straighter. "You need to stop dropping by unannounced. You scared away another one."

"I'm guessing she'll return around tea time. His highness will need help to feed himself lunch."

"Sod off."

Mercer snorted. "Try not to anger these women. They could easily eliminate you and make it look like an accident."

"Is that why you're here? You feel the need to offer someone protection? Or do you want to spring me? Do you need help on a job?"

Mercer didn't respond. Instead, he took a seat beside the bed and reached for the chart. He read the latest entries. The surgery went well. The inflammation was decreasing. The initial physical assessment showed an increased range of motion.

"At least Donovan brings those little cakes. And Bastian brings magazines and crossword puzzles."

Placing the chart back in its slot, Mercer let out a sigh. "How do you feel?" He knew his teammate well. It was no secret Hans' sense of humor and mouthiness often led to clashes between them, but beneath the surface friction, they were as tight as brothers. Hans was scared. If he didn't recover adequately, he wouldn't be able to serve as overwatch or conduct recon. The team would be a man down, and everything would change. Mercer found the notion rather disagreeable. "Are you able to do anything with that arm?"

"Perhaps you should ask the bird who just left." Seeing the annoyance on Mercer's face, Hans sobered. "It's coming along. The physical therapy starts up again at the end of the week. One of the therapists offered to make house calls."

"And you're certain you want to stay with your mum? We have room at the flat."

"Donovan already offered, but we're home. I might as well spend some time being at home. Plus, you met my mum. She won't take no for an answer, and I can't say I'm opposed to her home-cooked meals."

"Right." Mercer nodded, his mind drifting to other matters.

"Is everything all right?"

"Yes."

Hans scrutinized him for a moment. "Bollocks. If there's a job..."

"There isn't. We aren't taking any without you. Get well, soldier. That's an order."

"We aren't in the SAS anymore. You can't order me around."

"Do you want to say that again?"

Hans made an overly exaggerated gulp. "No, sir."

The smile tugged at his lips. "Thanks, Jules."

Mercer nodded. "I'll make sure your bill is paid and the physical therapist is covered. Is there anything else in the meantime?"

"See if you can track down an attractive nursing assistant. I could use a sponge bath."

"Wanker."

TWO

After leaving the hospital, Mercer transferred additional funds to cover the rest of the medical expenses. The K&R specialists were often compensated handsomely for their work, but the money for Hans' recovery was basically blood money. The team had been hesitant to take it, but Mercer knew they'd need it. And as usual, he was right.

He exhaled, scanning the streets. He didn't want to go back to the flat. He spent every day going over the details related to his wife's murder. It didn't matter where they were. He always kept those files on hand in case an epiphany struck or new intel surfaced. But being in London, so close to where the crime was committed, amplified the helplessness and anger to an almost unbearable degree. Mercer needed to find answers before the pressure became too much and he exploded.

Ducking into the police station, he spoke to the officer at the front desk and took a seat. This was a familiar game. One he had grown accustomed to playing. The inspector assigned to his wife's case enjoyed making him wait as long as possible in the hopes Mercer would grow bored or frustrated and leave. As usual, that didn't happen, and inevitably, Inspector Brickle ushered Mercer to his desk.

"Mr. Mercer, I don't have anything new for you."

"Pity." Mercer dropped into a chair, having no intention of leaving until some sort of progress was made or the inspector agreed to reopen the investigation. "The Metropolitan Police Service really is nothing but a laughingstock."

"Watch your mouth."

"One of the private detectives I hired came to a very disconcerting conclusion. Do you care to hear it?"

"Not unless it involves your confession."

Feeling his fists clench, Mercer inhaled. Once he was calmer, he straightened his fingers. Unlike negotiating with kidnappers, this matter was personal, but he was determined to implement the same tactics he used when dealing with irrational and desperate men. Calm, firm reasoning was the only way to deal with self-aggrandizing sows.

"The spatter patterns weren't indicative of a hasty, violent attack. There was no spatter on the walls or ceiling. Your theory doesn't fit the crime."

Brickle reached for a legal pad. "So the killer wasn't rushed. He took his time. Any idea how long he was there? Minutes? Hours?"

"Not more than thirty minutes. The attack itself happened in less than five." Mercer recalled the conclusions Alexis Parker relayed to Bastian. "Michelle was bleeding out when I arrived home. He stabbed her and left."

"He." Brickle jotted something down. "Do you have a description?"

"We've been through this."

"Humor me. You wanted to rehash the crime."

Mercer sensed this was a trap, but the tiniest part of him always held out hope. "He was strong. Trained in the art of killing. He paralyzed her first to keep her from fighting back."

"Seems like you have it all figured out. Why wait so long to come forward with this?"

Every muscle in Mercer's body went taut. "It took time to find a competent detective who could find some clues in the mess you left behind. If it weren't for you and the rest of your pathetic lot, maybe you would have realized something was amiss and paid attention to the evidence. Perhaps you wouldn't have tromped through my house and destroyed what little hope we had of finding a usable shoeprint or fingerprint or any bloody clue as to this man's identity," Mercer spat, moments away from losing control. So much for calm reasoning.

Brickle watched Mercer's chest heave, his eyes darting back and forth as if enjoying a match at Wimbledon. "Let's say I buy this theory of yours. You realize what you're suggesting sounds like nothing more than a conspiracy. Do you think the killer asked us to cover his tracks?"

Something dark came over Mercer. "It's possible."

"Are you daft? Who has the kind of clout necessary to do something like that?" The inspector arched an eyebrow. "Perhaps a decorated military officer with ties to several policing agencies? Would that be someone you would suspect of manipulating the Met in such a manner?"

"Stop twisting my words. I wasn't there. If I never went to the bloody market that afternoon, I could have protected her." The wound in his chest ripped open at the flood of memories. "I just gave you an accurate profile. The killer was careful and strong. He was trained. He knew where and how to strike. He made certain she couldn't fight back and no one was around to hear her screams or see him escape. He fucking killed her, and you let him get away."

The eye roll was followed by a derisive snort. The inspector's perspective was so clouded by his preconceived notions he refused to believe Mercer's pain was real. Instead, Brickle believed this was a twisted and deranged game being performed for the killer's perverse pleasure—Julian's perverse pleasure.

"I gather someone with special ops training would be able to pull off the type of crime you're suggesting. And correct me if I'm wrong, but forensics speculated she didn't struggle because she knew her attacker. What do you make of that?"

Mercer stared at him. "You need to listen to me. That is precisely what I'm saying."

"You're saying what exactly, Mr. Mercer? That someone just like you could stab someone to death and get away with it?"

Mercer's eyes went dark. He knew the police would be no help. Once again, his hope was crushed. "Do you want to find out?"

"Stop threatening and make a move. Or are you a coward? Maybe you only enjoy hurting defenseless women."

Ignoring the pathetic attempt at being goaded, Mercer held the inspector's gaze. "I would like to see the original photos taken at the scene, along with the technician's report."

"You already have copies."

"I want to see the originals."

"Suspects aren't usually given access to investigative materials."

"Need I remind you the Commissioner ordered all information be disclosed to me regarding this matter?"

"You're lucky you have friends in high places. If you didn't, you'd be behind bars." The inspector was smart enough to know Mercer wouldn't leave until the request was fulfilled, but he had a few other things to take care of first. The way Brickle saw it, the longer Mercer remained in the police station, the better. "I'll fetch it for you. Anything else?" he asked sarcastically.

Mercer remained silent, and the inspector disappeared down the corridor.

Despite the lack of evidence, everything about Michelle Mercer's murder pointed to her husband. The wound tracks matched a knife found in Mercer's closet, and the neighbors claimed Julian was the only person they saw enter and leave the house that day. To top it off, after Michelle's murder, the SAS determined Mercer suffered from mental instability and violent tendencies and forced him into an early retirement.

Not to mention, most women were killed by their husbands. That was simply a fact. However, the circumstances led Mercer to an unsettling conclusion. It was the only one that fit. Someone he knew and trusted killed Michelle. He had to find out who it was. Perhaps something in the official record could help him identify the killer.

Forty-five minutes later, Brickle returned with a dusty cardboard box. Inside were the officers' notepads, crime scene photos, and bagged evidence from the scene. Brickle placed the box on top of his desk. "You may review the items but only under careful supervision. I know precisely what's inside the box. If anything goes missing, it will be considered tampering and possibly obstruction. I'd hate to bring an upstanding chap like you up on charges."

The tunnel vision kicked in, and Mercer's focus

went to the box and the secrets it contained. For hours, he examined the bagged items and scanned the photos with a magnifying glass, but they were exactly the same as the copies he had at home. He read the reports word for word, but they were just as he remembered. His government and military connections, along with Bastian's help, allowed him to procure all the official data related to the crime. The only things he didn't possess were the physical evidence and the internal memos.

As he went from bag to bag, soldiering through the bloody towels and rags, the clothes Michelle wore that dark day, and the other random items which found their way into police evidence, he struggled to recall details. Something must have been amiss, but he didn't remember. All he remembered was her. He put down an evidence bag and pressed his hands to his face. He felt sick and dizzy. He wanted to vomit and sob and scream, but he'd settle for beating the shit out of the arrogant police inspector. Fortunately, he knew better.

"You forgot something." Brickle's smug tone tore through Mercer's attempt at calming his raging emotions.

"What?"

Brickle fished a bag of official notepads from beneath a cardboard divider at the bottom of the box. "It's best you look through these now so I can go another few months without you darkening my doorstep."

Mercer reached for the bag, eyeing it with curiosity. He barely remembered seeing the notebooks before today. Sliding open the bag, he pulled out the stack and placed them on top of the desk. Selecting one at random, he flipped through the pages. It was an account taken by the responding officer. While Mercer scanned the pages, searching for a hidden gem which had gotten lost in the mix, Brickle picked up one of the other notepads and began to read.

"If you can't beat 'em, join 'em," Brickle said.

A third of the way through the fourth notepad, Mercer stopped. His tone remained low and calm, which the inspector found far more frightening than the usual barely contained rage. "Where are the pages?"

"What?"

"The pages." Mercer held open the pad, shoving it in the inspector's face. "You tore them out when I wasn't looking, didn't you? You thought it'd be an excellent excuse to detain me for the next day or two." He glared at the inspector. "Where are they?"

Brickle's gaze went to the opened book. "Let me see that."

Letting out a huff, Mercer dropped the notepad on the desk and folded his arms over his chest. "Did you stuff them down your trousers?"

Brickle flipped through the rest of the notepad, returning to the spot where three pages had been torn out. Reaching into the box, he flipped through the inventory, checking for any notes. "Are the rest intact?"

"As far as I'm aware. Did you tear out the pages?"

"You might not like me, but that's a serious accusation. And one to which I take great offense." Brickle keyed in something and lifted his desk phone. "I need to speak to Detective Chief Inspector Yancy." He paused. "First thing in the morning then." Hanging up the phone, he assessed Mercer but remained silent. Instead, he scanned the remainder of the notepads, finding a second one missing several pages. He narrowed his eyes, knowing damn well the security specialist hadn't gone through the second damaged notebook yet. "It appears someone else might have tampered with the evidence."

Mercer held the man's gaze. Then he stood and placed a business card with nothing but a phone number on the inspector's desk. "Contact me as soon as those pages are located or when you have an explanation as to why or how this happened."

THREE

Mercer's mind was reeling. He wasn't an optimist by any stretch of the imagination. This discrepancy might be nothing more than a clerical error, or, more than likely, some corrupt bobbies covering the mishandling of the crime scene by altering their reports and removing the contradiction from existence. Still, as he walked out of the police station, he sensed the slightest bit of doubt in Inspector Brickle's resolve. Perhaps the incompetent copper was reconsidering Mercer's theory.

Letting out an aggravated growl, he let himself into the flat. "Bastian?"

"He's out," Donovan replied. "He left as soon as I got here."

"When'd you get back?"

"Two and a half hours ago. Is everything all right? Is it Hans?"

"Hans is fine. Cheeky as ever." Mercer went into the kitchen to make a cup of tea. While he waited for the kettle, he filled Donovan in on recent developments.

"What do you think the police are hiding?"

"Their incompetence."

"I'm not sure they'd bother attempting to conceal it. Surely, you must have read through those notes before."

"I don't remember. I think I saw the booklets before, but I don't know that I read them or even flipped through them. Maybe I didn't think they were important."

"From the start, you've been convinced everything is important. This isn't your oversight. It might be theirs." Donovan analyzed the dark puffy circles and two days' worth of beard growth on the commander's face. "You must be knackered. Why don't you knock off. I'll go through the files to see if you have copies of their notes or a report explaining these discrepancies."

"You were out all night, closing down the pubs, I presume."

Donovan worked the grin off his face. "Not exactly, mate. I had a pretty quiet night, got plenty of rest and a bit of exercise."

"Fine, but tell Bastian to wake me when he arrives."

"Anything else?"

Mercer picked up his cup and moved toward the bedroom. "See what you can dig up on DCI Argus Yancy. His notepad was a few pages light. I'm guessing the other dodgy one belongs to his partner."

After taking a few sips, he stripped down and settled into bed. His muscles felt tight from lack of use. He tried to remember what it was like to feel normal. Sadly, he couldn't remember. He just knew a part of him missed it, and it was something he'd never fully reclaim. Closing his eyes, he shifted onto his side and forced the voices to quiet.

His body and mind were too tired to dream.

Perhaps his subconscious understood he couldn't withstand another round of torment. For once, he slept soundly. Several hours later, he was roused by metallic scraping. It wasn't loud enough to fully draw him into consciousness, but it was enough of a nuisance to direct his subconscious mind to other matters.

Someone was watching Julian Mercer. He felt it whenever he left the flat. Sometimes, he'd feel it at the pubs or on his way home. It didn't always happen, but it happened frequently enough to cause concern. Mercer found it even more troubling that he never spotted the source.

The scrape sounded again. He shot up in bed, convinced whoever was watching him was here. Snatching the handgun from the holster beside the bed, he moved out of the bedroom and toward the source of the sound. Throwing open the door, he aimed at Bastian.

"Bloody key's stuck." Bastian twisted and yanked to get it out. "Maybe we should change the locks. Did someone steal your trousers?"

"We have a problem."

"Is it a trouser thief?"

Mercer backed away from the door to shower and dress. By the time he emerged, Donovan had briefed Bastian about the evidence discrepancy. Bastian was at the computer, using a backdoor into the police department's servers to search for relevant files. Most things were computerized, but the K&R specialists didn't know if the officers' notebooks were included in the online filing system.

Settling in beside Donovan, Mercer reached into the file box and pulled out a stack of documents. He skimmed the pages. Most were reports provided to him by the various private investigators he hired.

With the exception of Alexis Parker, an American federal agent, none of the private eyes contributed anything of value.

Mercer glanced at the untraceable burner and considered giving Parker a ring. "I need a new phone. I gave Inspector Brickle my number, and I don't want him to be able to track it."

"Spares are in the cabinet to your left," Bastian said.

Mercer retrieved a new phone, forwarding the calls from his previous one to the new one. If the inspector decided to trace his location, it would only lead him to the phone. Mercer entered Parker's number but didn't press send. "Did you get anything off the vehicles or plates?"

Bastian shook his head. "The killer was careful. I dropped by the MI5 offices and asked a few friends to take a look at the surveillance feeds. If they were tampered with, we'll know soon."

Mercer dropped the phone and returned to the file box. When he and Donovan reached the bottom, finding no copies of the notepads or an explanation for the missing pages, he got up to pace. The missing pages were his new obsession.

"Someone destroyed those pages and kept me from reading them or learning about them prior to today."

"Are you certain that's not the paranoia talking, Jules?" Bastian asked.

Donovan looked grim. "I hate to say it, mate, but it sounds plausible."

Mercer leaned over Bastian's shoulder to see what the analyst was working on. "When you're done researching, print a dossier on DCI Yancy." He scooped the phone off the table. "I'm going to call Parker."

"And ask her what? I told her we could handle this

and she was no longer indebted to you."

"That wasn't your place. And this isn't about some debt." Taking the phone, Mercer stalked into the kitchen. His team would be able to hear him, but he wouldn't have to see their concerned expressions or deal with Bastian's whispered insistence to be nice. Mercer worked with Parker on two separate occasions. She didn't expect him to be nice.

When she finally answered, he said, "I need you to dig into some members of the Metropolitan Police Service, specifically DCI Yancy and whoever his partner was at the time of my wife's murder."

"What am I looking for?"

"Anything. You've exchanged intel with the Met before. They must have some records they'd be willing to share."

She cleared her throat. "About that, I'm not with the OIO anymore."

"Then what bloody good are you?"

"Mercer," she began, but he disconnected before she could say anything else.

Storming into the living room, he stopped his procession as soon as he saw the guilt written on Bastian's face. "You knew. If she's not an American agent, how can she possibly help us?"

"Jules, when you first met her, she was nothing more than a security consultant. She has resources and friends in the right places. Her new position affords her better access than what she was granted by the U.S. government. Don't discount her abilities." Bastian turned back to the computer screen. "Just leave her alone. This is our fight."

"My fight," Mercer corrected.

"Anything ever turn up with these articles?" Donovan held up the manila envelope which contained newspaper clippings and a note from

Carlton Rhoade, a newspaper mogul in Chicago who claimed Michelle's murder was just one in a string of homicides, but after perusing the cases and reading the clippings, it appeared to be another dead end. "Perhaps I should drop by the police station and ask about another of these incidents. See if any other notes are missing. What do you think?"

"Do as you like." Mercer took a seat opposite Bastian and reached for a tablet. He wanted to know everything about the bobbies involved in his wife's case, particularly DCI Yancy and Inspector Brickle. If they were corrupt, there would be a pattern of mishandled evidence and unsolved cases. "But be careful. I believe we are under surveillance."

"By whom?" Bastian asked.

"I'll use caution." Donovan went to the window and peeked out the blinds. "Have you spotted anyone?"

"No, but I feel it." Mercer tapped on the screen. He had to know who these cops were, where they went, who they screwed, the schools their children attended, and any exploitable weaknesses they might have. "If you need assistance, we'll be there."

Nodding, Donovan reached for his weapon, checked the laser sight, chambered a round, and went to the door. It didn't hurt he was one of the best shooters to come out of the Special Air Service. Once he was gone, Mercer and Bastian worked the rest of the day in silence. The only sound inside the apartment was the hum of the printer and the click of the stapler as they tacked pages to the wall. Finding the killer was their mission and entire focus until Hans was back with them. It was about bloody time Michelle's murder took precedence.

FOUR

Argus Yancy headed the homicide task force of the Metropolitan Police Service. He was fifty-two years old, giving him an entire decade on Mercer. He was divorced, had three children, two of which were married and the third was completing a doctorate at university. He lived alone and appeared to be nothing more than a miserable son of a bitch. His life, like many in law enforcement, was the job.

From what Mercer gathered, Yancy never investigated. His signature was at the bottom of several official documents and reports, but those were submitted by inspectors and officers under his command. He issued the public statement concerning Michelle's murder, but it was nothing more than the company line. So why was Yancy's notepad missing three pages?

"He probably tore out those sheets to wipe his arse," Bastian said.

"What about the other damaged notepad?" Mercer stared at the array of intelligence they compiled.

"That one belonged to Lee Farnsworth. He was nothing but a lowly officer. You really missed the mark in your belief they were partners."

"What do we have on Farnsworth?"

"Not much, I'm afraid. He was an apprentice, still in training at the time of the event. That was Farnsworth's first violent crime scene. He canvassed the neighborhood and took statements from your neighbors."

"Farnsworth knew something or spoke to someone who did, and Yancy concealed it." Snatching the file out of Bastian's hand, Mercer flipped through the pages, hoping to find Farnsworth's personal information. "I need to speak to him directly."

"You'll need to find a medium. Farnsworth was killed two weeks later."

"How?"

"The police responded to reports of a brawl. When they arrived, Farnsworth was in a coma. Based on the call, the police deduced he tried to break up the fight, took a hit to the back of the head, and never woke up."

"Convenient. Who killed him?"

"By the time back-up arrived, the place was cleared out. The tavern owner across the street provided a description of the men involved, but it was dark. She didn't see much. And it wasn't caught on camera."

"Bugger." Dropping the file to the table, Mercer leaned against the wall and tried to make sense of these events. "This has to be more than a string of bad luck."

"Bad luck, unfortunate coincidence, call it what you will, but it stinks to high heaven." Bas grabbed a handful of crisps. "I'm sorry, Jules."

Mercer looked confused.

"You've been through a lot, and there is no easy solution."

"I know."

"We'll figure it out."

"We haven't so far." Mercer waved a hand at the mess of paperwork. "And this is probably nothing more than worthless drivel." He squeezed his eyes closed and bumped his back against the wall. After a moment, he opened his eyes. "Farnsworth's dead, but Yancy's not. He's going to tell us precisely what was ripped out of those notepads."

*   *   *

"Let me know if you spot him," Mercer said into the comm. Donovan was positioned across from Argus Yancy's tiny, two bedroom cottage, serving as lookout while Mercer broke inside. "And that he's alone. Our chat needs to be private."

"Yes, sir."

Mercer glanced around the patch of grass in the back, seeing nothing but the tall privacy fence. Yancy was the only one in the neighborhood with a fence.

It didn't take much effort to hoist himself over. Taking his time, Mercer went to the back door and knelt beside it. His gloved hands worked the tools into the top lock, repeating the process a second time before the door opened.

"I'm in," Mercer declared.

Bastian remained at the flat, tapped into the police frequencies. A break-in at a cop's home would take priority, but no one had reported anything suspicious. "Careful, he has a security system."

Mercer moved to the beeping panel on the wall. Thanks to their research, he already knew the override code. As he disarmed the system, loud barking sounded from another room, followed by the skittering of nails on the tile floor. "And a dog."

"Shit," Donovan cursed.

The last thing Mercer wanted to do was kill the creature. If he couldn't make peace with the animal or trap it in a room, he wouldn't have a choice. Based on those ferocious barks, the dog would surely tear him apart.

Aiming at the source of the sound, he took an uneasy step closer to the back door and waited. The frantic scraping grew nearer until a white and tan spaniel burst into the room. Its tail wagging so hard its hindquarters shook from side to side.

Snorting, Mercer holstered the weapon as the dog bounded toward him. Once it was within reach, it stopped, let out a loud, deep bark which shook the room, and sniffed in Mercer's direction. Curling his fingers under, Mercer held his hand out and knelt down. The dog gave his hand a thorough sniffing, decided the intruder was friendly, and put her front paws on his leg in order to lick his face.

"Enough of that," Mercer said, scratching her behind the ears. "You're a pathetic excuse for a guard dog. I hope you know that."

"Jules?" Donovan asked. "It's quiet out here. Everything okay?"

"Fine. It's a spaniel. Its bark is worse than its bite." The dog leapt, licking Mercer's chin as he stood. "Its tongue might be the only deadly thing about it."

"I thought dogs were supposed to be good judges of character," Bastian remarked. "That one is clearly broken."

"Probably from living with Yancy." Mercer wiped his gloved hands on his trousers and surveyed the room. The dog looked up at him and whined. He opened the back door, and the dog went to play in the enclosed yard. That explained the fence.

"I'm sorry, mate. There was no mention of a pet,"

Bastian said.

"Let's hope that's the only surprise." Mercer assessed the living room, glancing briefly at the photos on the mantel. This would be the last room he searched. Moving down the hallway, he entered the master bedroom and looked around. "Any suggestions on how to open the safe?"

"We'll run through the usual combinations," Bastian said. "Tell me when you're ready."

Thirteen attempts later, Mercer stood in front of the opened safe. Inside was a firearm, two boxes of ammunition, Yancy's will, the deed to the property, insurance information, a marriage license, a copy of the divorce papers, a passport, and what appeared to be some family heirlooms. Mercer sifted through the tiny jeweled trinkets, deciding the contents of the safe were nothing more than rubbish. They didn't provide any insight into why Yancy might be protecting Michelle's killer.

He continued his search, investigating every nook and cranny as he went. Yancy didn't have any dark secrets, and if he did, they weren't in plain sight. After checking for hidden compartments in the furniture, anything hidden under or inside the mattress, and examining the closet for a false back, Mercer repeated the search in the second bedroom.

This room was nothing more than a guestroom. The furniture was empty. The closet contained a winter coat, Christmas decorations, and a few containers of pet supplies.

Checking the time, Mercer entered the bathroom. In the cabinet, he found a tube of lubricant and a dusty box of condoms. "Does Yancy have any lovers?"

"None that I'm aware," Bastian replied, "but we didn't know about the dog either."

"The bastard's hopeful." Mercer found a

prescription pill bottle and read the physician's name to Bastian. As he finished his search of the bathroom and went to the kitchen, he heard the faint sound of a car door. The dog enthusiastically barked, and Mercer cringed. The creature had a big mouth. It was going to give away his position. "Donovan, any sign of the detective?"

"Negative. The neighbor to the east just came home. Yancy should be arriving soon, within the next twenty minutes, depending on traffic. You need to hurry it up."

Mercer opened and closed several cupboards. "I'm not in a rush." The barking stopped, and Mercer let out a breath. "Let me know if any other neighbors show up, preferably before the barking alerts them to the fact something is wrong."

The kitchen didn't turn up anything of interest, so Mercer returned to the living room. The detective's laptop was on the coffee table. Mercer waited for the screen to light up before removing a memory stick from his pocket. After plugging in the external device, he followed the prompts and checked to make sure it was connected to the internet.

"We're in," Bastian whispered. Sometimes the analyst forgot he wasn't on-site and could speak at a normal volume. "Copy his hard drive. While you do that, I'll execute the Trojan horse program so we can monitor his activity."

"Brilliant." While the files were copied to the drive, Mercer examined the items in the living room. Yancy had photos of his ex-wife, their children, and his children's families covering his walls and mantelshelf. A pile of dog toys and a dog bed littered the floor. For someone who might be on the take, Yancy didn't live large.

When the dog started to whine, Mercer opened the

back door. The dog scampered inside, jumping up in greeting before going to the water bowl in the kitchen. Mercer watched as the animal drank. It looked up at him expectantly, pawing at the empty food bowl.

Realizing the time, Mercer removed the external drive from the laptop and shut the computer. "Shouldn't Yancy be here by now? His pet is hungry."

"He should have arrived an hour ago," Donovan said. "Since we put him under surveillance, he's come straight home every night, with the exception of picking up supper. And that never takes more than fifteen minutes. This doesn't make sense. Are you sure you didn't trigger an alarm?"

"Negative." But despite his insistence, Mercer scanned the room for signs of hidden surveillance equipment.

"Let me see what's going on," Bastian said. "There was some chatter on the police frequencies earlier, but no word on it being a homicide. It shouldn't have delayed Yancy, but perhaps he stayed late to assist with the situation."

"What kind of situation?" Mercer asked.

"Some nutter called in a bomb threat. It's all over the news. I'm not sure if that's the cause of Yancy's delay, but if it is, I imagine he'll be quite late. What do you want to do, Jules?"

Mercer exhaled slowly, his shoulders tight. Waiting around was the last thing he wanted to do. "We'll retreat for now. I'll speak to him another time." He gave the cottage the quick once-over to make sure nothing appeared disturbed. The dog followed him every step of the way. When they made it back into the kitchen, the animal let out a whine. "You're one mouthy lass, aren't you?" Normally, he had to deal with Hans. Now he had this mutt. The dog whined again, pawing at her bowl.

Opening the container of kibble, Mercer sprinkled some into the dish. While the animal was distracted, he went out the back door and secured it in place before jumping the fence.

"I'll meet you at the car," Donovan said.

FIVE

"His financials don't show any discrepancies. I've checked everything from the time of Michelle's murder through the present. Yancy didn't take a payoff. His police file isn't exactly exemplary. He had a rather severe civilian complaint lodged against him and was placed on administrative probation for excessive violence. It looks like he sat through some mandated anger management," Bastian said, "but nothing indicates he's dirty. There are no open internal investigations concerning Yancy or his task force."

"What about his personal online activity?" Mercer asked.

Bastian gnawed on the end of some fruit leather. "He plays online poker and comes out about even. So we don't have any loan sharks or crime connections to worry about. Aside from that, he's listed on a few online dating sites, and he checks his kids' social media profiles religiously."

"That's not helpful."

"I hate to say it, mate, but those removed pages may very well be meaningless."

Fixing Bastian with an icy look, Mercer stepped away from the computer. "Dig deeper."

"Yes, sir."

While Bastian remained behind the computer screen, Mercer went through the news articles again. The crimes were similar, but the method of killing was different. The weapons were different. If these crimes were committed by the same person, the killer was smart and professional. Mercer thought of the men and teams he encountered, but his wife's murder was personal. Things that happened in the field weren't supposed to follow him home. Michelle wasn't a hired hit or another job. He knew it, felt it innately in his bones and his soul. Whoever killed her did so just to be cruel.

Forcing as much of the tension away as possible, Mercer tried to clear away the anger and the pain. He needed to think clearly. Rationally. The answer could be right here. He just needed to see it. *Focus on the commonalities*, his mind ordered. Since his team finagled copies of the other homicide reports, he took care to slowly peruse them. As he noted before, DCI Yancy signed off on each of the scenes. Other than that, the cases didn't follow a similar pattern. "Bleeding incompetent fool," Mercer muttered, castigating himself and his failures.

Returning to the dossier on Yancy, he picked up a printout of the detective's recent credit card charges. He wasn't averse to returning to Yancy's home to have a conversation, but maybe he should throw the detective off balance by popping up at a few of his favorite haunts first. Yancy's expenses were basic—stops for petrol, groceries, some fish and chip joints, and a couple of pubs. Two to be precise. One was near the police station. The other was on the east end. The second tavern wasn't remotely close to Yancy's home, work, or any of the other places he frequented.

Noting the oddity, Mercer checked the dates of the transactions. Yancy visited the tavern only when he had the next morning off. The copper wasn't making the trek across town when he had to get up early, which could mean one of several things. Perhaps he was a gentleman who didn't want to anger whatever bird he went home with by dashing off after their romp, or he couldn't work with a bloody hangover. Seeing this as a way to gain leverage, Mercer researched Lucie's Tavern. As far as he could tell, it was a legitimate business, at least on paper.

"I'm going out," Mercer declared.

Bastian looked up from the screen. "Where?"

"To the pub." He circled the name on the financial statement and put it on the table.

"Taking Donovan with you?"

Mercer shook his head. The long-range expert was helping Hans get settled, and Mercer didn't want to interfere. Furthermore, he didn't presume to need back-up. He just wanted to get the lay of the land. It was doubtful Yancy would show up tonight. He was scheduled for an early shift the next day.

Forty minutes later, Mercer parked outside the tavern. He studied the neighborhood. It wasn't posh or trendy, but strangely, he didn't sense a particularly strong criminal element either. Deciding to wait until dark to see if any ruffians crawled out of the sewers, he toyed with the idea of phoning Parker. The woman was a little too self-righteous and opinionated for his liking, but she promised to help. And she wouldn't go back on her word. Frankly, he sometimes wondered if the reason he found interacting with her so unappealing was because he knew how broken she was and didn't want to make it worse.

Swallowing his pride, he dialed the number and waited for her to answer. "Parker," he greeted.

"Mercer." Her tone matched his. She didn't speak again, waiting for him to say something. Why did she always make things so difficult? Hell, maybe he couldn't get along with her because she was too similar to him.

"I may have been hasty in terminating our arrangement."

"What do you want?" she asked.

For the next twenty minutes, he told her everything about the Chicago newsman who provided the articles, the case files and numbers to which they corresponded, and how he was led to believe whoever was responsible for those murders was also responsible for Michelle's death. "Bastian doesn't believe there is a connection. The modus operandi doesn't correlate. The crimes are dissimilar. Different weapons. Different everything."

"I know what modus operandi means."

"Do you speak Latin?"

"Wise ass. I didn't realize that was a required course at Cambridge," she retorted.

"This was a mistake."

"No doubt." She sighed. "Any similarities, aside from the fact some news guy told you they're linked?"

"Same bloody DCI. Yancy's task force investigated each scene. His name is on every report."

"I'm already looking into him. It can't hurt to look into these too. Send me the files and the official police reports. I've run out of favors with Interpol and New Scotland Yard."

"Okay."

"It wouldn't hurt if I could see those news articles too."

"I'll provide copies."

"Thanks. What's the newsman's name?"

"Carlton Rhoade."

She clicked her pen a few times and scribbled it down. "I'll get right on this. I'll let you know what I find."

"I'll await your call." He disconnected and stared into the growing darkness. He'd prefer fighting his own battles, but he'd use whatever resources were at his disposal to get the answers he sought. This time, he wasn't leaving London until he put that murdering arsehole in the ground. After sending a quick message to Bastian, relaying Parker's request, Mercer stepped out of the car. For a moment, he swore someone was watching him. He looked around, spotting no one in the vicinity. "I need a bloody drink."

The interior of the tavern was as he expected. The air was thick with smoke and the scent of distilled spirits. The tables were made of hardwood, scratched and pocked from years of use. The few vinyl booths were cracked. Two dozen people were drinking inside, and not a single football fan was among them. The dark atmosphere allowed anonymity, giving serious drinkers and those who sought to stay off the radar a place to meet. The hushed drone of quiet conversations filled the air, broken up by the sound of glasses striking tabletops.

Easing his way to the bar, Mercer warily eyed the men in the back corner. They were thin and twitchy, like a lot of addicts he'd seen. The handoff was almost impossible to miss, but when he chose to pay attention, not much went unnoticed. He wondered if Yancy had an addiction problem. Maybe the uptight bobby liked to use recreationally, or he got his rocks off by jostling the dealers.

Maneuvering to the opposite corner, Mercer took a

seat at the far end of the bar. He turned on the stool, resting his back against the wall. From here, he could see everything. No one could sneak up on him. Two seats down, a heavy-set man with a thick, unruly, ginger beard finished a stein of ale. He dropped a few quid on the bar and smiled brightly at the barmaid.

She scooped up the money. "Making it an early night, Piers?"

"Not much of a choice. I can't miss my train. Tube only runs so late."

"Take care," she called after him, her voice resonating with genuine concern and affection. Mercer's gaze shifted to the woman. Since when did people actually give a shit, particularly in a place like this? It wasn't until that moment that she noticed him and moved down the bar. "What's your poison?"

"Scotch, neat."

She grabbed a glass and gave a short pour, placing it in front of him. She squinted at the way he sat, assessing him for a moment before moving down the bar. Occasionally, she'd cast a sideways glance in his direction, wary of his presence. Mercer wondered why.

For several hours, he remained still. His only movement was the occasional sip from the glass. She refilled it at least three times, but this barmaid was stingy with her pours. They barely amounted to two shots. However, no one seemed to notice or mind.

The addicts in the back corner eventually slipped away. Mercer watched them go. No one else posed a threat, but in the low-lit pub, anything could happen. Murders could be arranged, contracts could be made, and drugs could be bought. So why did Yancy choose this tavern? He had to be dirty.

"You looking for someone?" She stopped to wipe the bar and top off his glass.

"No."

"Most people come in, sit down, drink as much as they need, and go. What's your story, mate?"

"There isn't enough liquor in the world."

"It might help if you drank faster."

"It might help if you were more generous."

She gave him a cheeky grin. "You noticed?"

"Yes."

She held out the bottle, silently asking if he wanted more added to his glass, but he shook his head. "Why are you sitting in my pub?"

"Your pub?"

"Did you read the sign on the door? This is Lucie's Tavern. Did you think it referred to the burly bloke at the register?"

"So you're Lucie?" Mercer didn't particularly care what her name was. However, he did care why she was taking such an interest. From the interactions he'd witnessed, she didn't know everyone by name. There were only a handful of regulars, most of whom were sloppy drunks who would piss themselves before the night was through. The rest would duck in for a few pints and head out.

"This is the part where you tell me your name."

"I assure you it isn't."

She smiled, cocking her head to the side. "I love a challenge." He finished his drink and reached into his wallet. It was time to go before she could ask any more questions. Before he could put the money on the counter, she shook her head and cleared away his glass. "First-timers drink free. You come back, I'm gonna need your name and cash. You might want to think twice about that."

Nodding, he stepped out of the tavern, aware of a few sets of eyes trailing him. On the way to his parked car, he detoured to a dead end alley and waited. If anyone on the street noticed, they'd think he ducked down there to take a leak. No one from the bar followed him, but the hair at the back of his neck prickled. Danger was near.

After adequate time passed, he stepped back onto the street. Most of the streetlamps were broken, but the headlights from passing cars provided ample illumination. He scanned the vicinity, catching a glimpse of someone in the shadows across the street. Dashing into oncoming traffic, he ignored the blaring car horn as he went in search of the predator.

The alcove where Mercer thought he saw someone was empty, but he caught the faintest whiff of a clove cigarette. Someone had been here. Watching. Waiting. The alcove was little more than a barred doorway to an electronics repair store. For someone to have been standing here and escape undetected, he must have had a route already mapped. Whoever was watching Mercer was trained in the art of stealth. Otherwise, Mercer would have seen where the bastard went, unless this shadow could walk through walls. Just to be sure, he gave the bars a hard yank and checked the area for places to hide.

Shaking it off as a trick of the lights, he returned to his parked car. His eyes caught movement at the tavern door, and he watched one of the drunks teeter away. When the man was no longer in sight, Mercer turned back to the spot across the street, still aware of a nearby presence, but no one was there. Whoever was watching him couldn't be more than an apparition. Pondering his own sanity, he unlocked the car.

He'd barely gone a block when he heard an odd clicking. The sound was familiar. Something he'd heard before. Glancing at the gauges, he noticed the check engine light was illuminated. He brought the vehicle to a stop in the parking lane. His gaze went to the side mirror, and that's when he noticed a flashing red halo reflecting off a puddle below the vehicle.

Mercer watched it blink in time with the clicking. Throwing open the door, he lunged out of the seat. Before his body hit the pavement, the pressure sensor detected his absence and triggered an explosion. A ball of heat and flame propelled him higher into the air, and he landed hard on the asphalt, rolling to put the embers out before the flames could lick his skin.

"Bloody hell." His gaze swept the streets and sidewalks. Someone planted the bomb. Did the assailant stick around to watch the detonation? If Mercer hadn't noticed the clicking, would the bomb have gone off at a predetermined time or after the odometer reached a set distance? It had a pressure sensor, so it must have been planted while he was inside the tavern or else it would have detonated when he arrived.

He searched through the drizzling rain and the dense fog. When he didn't spot anyone, he reached into his pocket and pulled out his phone. "Bas, I need the footage from outside Lucie's Tavern. Now."

"How about a please?"

"Now," he growled. "Someone planted a device. They tried to light up the car with me in it."

"Did you see who it was?"

"If I did, I'd be having this conversation with him instead."

A moment later, the phone rang.

"Careful what you wish for," a voice warned, and the line went dead.

Mercer scanned his surroundings. The bomber was watching him, but he couldn't pick him out of the growing crowd. The man was a ghost.

SIX

It had been hours since the explosion. The team scoured the footage and read the preliminary reports. Their goal was to identify the bomber, but it was a fruitless endeavor.

The phone rang, and Mercer gave it a wary glance. The only person who had that number was Inspector Brickle, but the display listed *unknown* as the caller. He let it ring again, eyeing Bastian. "Give out my number?"

"Of course not." Bas's fingers flew over the keyboard as he prepared to run a trace.

"Hello?" Mercer pressed the speaker button.

A voice responded, "Close call. You really ought to be more careful, commander. Have you forgotten everything you were taught?"

"Who is this?"

Bastian hit a few keys, hoping to get a location and identity. Donovan moved to the window, scanning the exterior of the flat. No one was in sight, but to be certain, he went out the back to check the perimeter.

"You'll figure it out eventually," the voice replied.

"What do you want?" Mercer snapped.

The caller laughed. "I'll see you around, Julian."

Abruptly, the call ended.

Mercer turned to Bastian. "Who the hell was that?"

"I've got nothing." He showed Mercer the screen. "The call didn't bounce off any towers, and it wasn't routed through the internet."

"SAT phone," Mercer concluded, glaring at the device as if it betrayed him. "Brickle must be working with the bomber, or he is the bomber. The inspector is the only one who has this number."

"Your phone number could be ascertained through other means. It doesn't mean the inspector is involved."

But Mercer didn't bother listening to his friend's rationale. "Maybe Brickle planted the IED last night, but I would have recognized him."

"Do you hear yourself, Jules? Nothing in the inspector's record indicates he has experience with explosives."

Brickle's financials didn't show any suspicious activity. His service record was exemplary, but Mercer never liked the man. It wasn't beyond the realm of reason to think the bobby might have something to do with the mysterious caller or last night's car bomb. The evidence pointed to a connection of sorts.

Donovan returned, entering through the front door and being greeted by the business ends of Mercer's and Bastian's handguns. "Easy, gentlemen, it's only me. No sign of anyone outside." He jerked his chin at the phone. "What did he want? Was he calling to gloat?"

"Most likely," Bastian replied.

Mercer's mind went back to the prior evening. "We've seen devices like this before." He put the MI5 report down. "The pressure plate was an added measure, but I don't understand the one second delay."

"Oversight," Donovan suggested.

Mercer shrugged. Bastian had gone over the surveillance videos, as had their contacts at MI5. Even the police investigated, but the image was blurry. The man remained cloaked and used the side of the car to conceal himself from the closest camera. He moved like a jungle cat, silent and deadly, and not at all like Inspector Brickle.

"He was watching. I saw movement across the street." Mercer squeezed his eyes closed, recalling everything from the previous evening. "But he bloody vanished into thin air."

"Thick air," Bastian corrected. "He used the fog to shroud his retreat."

"He didn't retreat. Every move was tactical." Mercer went to the window and glanced out the blinds. "Ever since we established ourselves here, someone's been following me. I've never spotted the bastard, but I feel him." He turned around and looked at his teammates. "Anything to report? Now's the time."

Donovan shook his head. Bastian shrugged.

Mercer went into the bedroom. He didn't have much. The team always traveled light. His belongings fit easily in a duffel, and the bulk of the intel concerning Michelle's murder filled a couple of boxes.

"We need to relocate." Mercer returned to the main room after packing his possessions. "It'd be best if I distance myself from you."

"Jules, that isn't wise. Someone's after us."

Mercer gave his best friend a wicked smile. "Not us. Me."

"You don't know that."

"Don't I? The bomber came after me. The call was to me." He narrowed his eyes at the device on the table. "He knows me by name. It makes sense to assume I'm his target."

"He referred to you as commander," Bastian pointed out. "He must know all of us."

"That means we know him," Donovan added. "We just need to identify him."

"That could take time. Time we don't have." Mercer thought through various plans of action. "The problem is Hans." He pocketed a new phone and filled his wallet with two sets of fake IDs, matching credit cards, and a few hundred quid. "He can't defend himself, and he's at his mum's. I won't tolerate civilian casualties. She needs protection. At the present, they both do."

"I'll stay with them," Donovan promised.

"Seriously, Jules, don't you think we need a better plan? We have no idea who's tracking you or why. This is premature," Bastian said, even as he removed the intel from the wall and placed it inside a box. "Splitting up is a bad idea. Divide and conquer and all that rubbish. You're being reactive. This could be precisely what the wanker wants."

Mercer grabbed a box and placed some files inside. "I'm being practical." He was tracking his wife's killer. He didn't have time to deal with some nutter with a vendetta. "We're stuck in this godforsaken hellhole. We can't go to ground, so we're doing the next best thing." Bastian opened his mouth to protest, but Mercer silenced him with a single look. "We do not know enough yet, but we work with what we have. He's been tracking me. Last night, he made a feeble attempt at eliminating me. I won't stay here and put you at risk. Until we know more, it's best to separate. I have to distance myself for now."

"Okay," Donovan replied. "I'll keep an eye on Hans."

"He won't like having a babysitter," Bastian remarked.

Donovan smiled. "I'll tell him Jules threw me out. He'll believe it."

Bastian pointed at the long-distance tactician. "Stay in radio communication. Call if things go tits up."

"And try to keep the company to a minimum," Mercer warned. "The fewer strangers with access to Hans' home, the better."

"That might be a tough sell. Hans' mum has a welcome home party planned, and let's not forget the various birds he's inevitably shagging," Donovan said.

"Do your best."

Going into the other room, Donovan went to pack his things.

"I'm so glad I leased this bloody flat for a six month stretch," Bastian muttered. "I was starting to think having something permanent was a nice change of pace." He shook the crumbs from a bag of crisps into his mouth. "Until we know more, I'll do the usual room rotation at a few of the dodgier joints. Where are you headed, Jules?"

"I don't know yet. We need new vehicles. We should use aliases to get them. It's only a matter of time before this bastard tries again. If he can't locate me, he might come for one of you. I assume he's done his homework."

"Do you have any idea who it might be?"

"Could be anyone."

"We've only worked a few local jobs, but I'll see if any of the kidnappers we've dealt with are believed to be operating in the area. Aside from that, it stands to reason it could be one of the bobbies you've harassed. Ever since we arrived in London, you've done nothing but poke at them. Assuming someone intentionally tampered with the evidence and investigation notes, the culprit must realize you're on to him and wants you to stop. He might have nicked your number off Brickle's desk without the inspector even noticing."

"Assuming it isn't Brickle. I always knew they were a corrupt lot."

"It seems that way. The smart thing to do is back off until we learn more." He looked at Mercer, knowing the only way the commander would back down would be if he was six feet under. "Just be careful who you rattle."

"Don't reach out to military intelligence for help with the police. Your contacts have proven useful when we are conducting negotiations or need access to government information, but they know too much about what I'm doing and thinking. If it's one of them, we don't want to make this any easier than it already is."

"Now you're being paranoid."

"It isn't paranoia." Mercer finished boxing up the items. "Until I get situated, I need you to keep these safe. Will you do that for me, Bas?"

"Yes. What should I do if Parker calls?"

"When you get a chance, ring her from a new line and tell her I'll be in touch."

Bastian nodded and watched Mercer leave. "Yep, definitely paranoid."

SEVEN

The first thing Mercer did was take a deep breath. This wasn't an enemy encampment or the sandbox. This was a different kind of battlefield—an urban jungle. He'd been in enough conflicts and battles to have a general idea of the equipment required, but first, he needed to tune himself into his environment. That included the weather, the traffic, the bystanders, and the dangers. All of it.

For a moment, he did nothing but stand on the sidewalk, watching the patterns, taking in the comingled smells of exhaust, foods, perfumes, and human waste, and listening for anything that stood out. The roar of the passing bus, the sounds of the cars stuck in traffic, bits of conversations, a barking dog, the hum of a power generator, and differing sounds of footfalls on the pavement. Nothing stood out. Nothing indicated he was being hunted.

Remaining alert, he set out to the west. He didn't have a destination in mind. Tactically, it would be best to set up a stronghold before planning his next move, but he knew the sooner he found a place to stay, the sooner he'd have to vacate. Being in one place too long would give the hunter time to find him, and he wasn't making that mistake again.

Bloody fool, he thought. They'd only been in London for two weeks the first time he felt someone's eyes on him. When he couldn't find the source of his unease, he let Bastian convince him it was paranoia brought about by acute stress from being back home, dealing with the possibility his team may never be whole again should Hans' surgeries prove useless, and his sleepless obsession with finding his wife's murderer. It was a lot for anyone to handle, and it had been years since Mercer was firing on all cylinders. But he should have known better. He should have trusted his sixth sense.

At first, the unsettling sensation happened rather infrequently. But as time went on, it happened more and more until it was a constant any time he stepped outside. Bastian had exterior security measures in place, and on Mercer's word, motion and heat sensors were installed along with hidden surveillance cameras. No one suspicious was ever caught on camera. Until the explosion last night, it appeared as if Mercer was haunted by a ghost.

However, ghosts couldn't rig pipe bombs to the gas tank of an automobile or wire the detonator to the odometer so it would explode after two kilometers. And they couldn't use a pressure plate as a back-up to activate the device. If it hadn't been for the lag time, Mercer wouldn't have survived. As it was, he had a few burns and charred clothing from the blast to serve as a reminder of his mistake.

He continued to make his way through the city on foot. A double-decker bus with a large tour group stopped on the corner. He watched the tourists aim their phones and cameras at a gothic piece of architecture before clicking away. Had the hunter stumbled upon him by chance, like the tourists and the building on the corner, or had he been tracking Mercer for some time?

It was nearly impossible to say. The K&R team moved around frequently. If someone was following them, by the time their location was discovered, the security specialists would have moved on. Most cases didn't last more than a few days. The ones that took longer were few and far between.

Mercer never paid for anything lavish out of a named account. Hans' medical expenses were covered by a numbered account which traced back to a fictitious corporation. Even the flat Bastian rented wasn't paid directly by them, but they'd been sloppy. Mercer had made purchases with his own credit card several times, and he was certain Bastian and Donovan had done the same. They didn't realize they were in jeopardy. His team believed this was a safe place. To Bastian, Donovan, and Hans, this was home.

After hours of walking in circles, Mercer bought a pass and waited on the platform for the train. He could ride around for a bit. He needed time to think, and being in an enclosed car limited the number of potential enemies. It also made a sudden disappearance or escape practically impossible. If someone followed him on board, he would notice. And he would address the situation.

Once he was confident no one on the train posed a threat, he allowed himself to relax. He stayed in the back, as far away as he could get from anyone else. As the countryside whooshed past, Mercer thought about the coppers to which he'd spoken.

Someone within the police force or another

government agency was actively helping to conceal the identity of Michelle's murderer. The missing pages assured him of this, even if the evidence was inconclusive. His quest to speak to DCI Yancy failed twice, and during his two most recent visits to the police station, first when he spoke to Brickle and the second time right after the explosion, Yancy was conveniently unavailable. The copper had to know something, which left questions in Mercer's mind. Was the car bomb connected to his wife's murder? Was the killer afraid Mercer was getting too close? Were the car bombing and ominous phone calls nothing more than distraction tactics? DCI Yancy was the key. He had to pin the man down for a chat.

EIGHT

"Julian, listen to me," Alexis Parker said, her voice full of something he couldn't quite discern over the staticky line, "Bastian told me about the car bomb. I know you don't want to hear this, but is it possible someone on your team is responsible for your wife's murder?"

"No," Mercer fidgeted with the door on the phone booth and glared at the idiot tourists lurking a few meters away. Phone booths were few and far between in most countries, but in London, photographs of the classic red booths were something travelers coveted.

"Hear me out. When I spoke to Bastian a few weeks ago, I asked him the same question and he said no, but..."

"Bastian did not kill my wife." Mercer clenched his fists so hard the muscles in his forearms threatened to break through the skin.

"No, I didn't mean th–"

"What do you mean?"

She fought to contain her own temper. "Think for one fucking minute. Who knows you've settled in

London? Who knows you're investigating your wife's murder? Who the hell knew where you were going? It wasn't a coincidence someone put a bomb under your car. Shit like that doesn't just happen. And the bomber called you right after and again the next day."

"Clearly, it can't be my team. We were all in the same bloody room."

"You're not listening. Whoever murdered Michelle knows you. He knows you're back in London. My guess is he figured you'd go down for her murder. He hoped you'd get locked up or fall into some deep, dark hole of despair. Instead, you left the SAS and the country. Now you're back, and that's causing problems. Who stood to gain by getting you out of the way originally?"

Mercer felt a tremble go through him. His chest constricted and everything went dim. "Why didn't he just kill me?" His throat was almost too tight to speak. "Why hurt her?"

"I don't know."

"Fuck."

"I'm sorry. We'll figure this out."

Unable to deal with the pointless platitude, Mercer slammed the phone onto the hook over and over again. He couldn't stop himself. It took nearly a minute before he was able to loosen his hand from the receiver. Taking a deep breath, he tugged on the hem of his jacket, righting himself before opening the door. The small group of tourists congregated nearby diverted their gaze and cowered as he went past. One of them was ballsy enough to record the ex-soldier's fit of rage, and without missing a beat, Mercer snatched the phone from the man's hand, tossed it to the ground, smashed it beneath his heel, and kept walking.

He needed to get off the street. He wasn't in any

condition to deal with the day-to-day annoyances of the city. Blowing out a breath, he continued his trek to his original destination, but Parker's words and logic wormed their way into his psyche. He always knew he was responsible. He was to blame for Michelle's death. Perhaps his hands didn't guide the blade, but the reason his wife was stabbed, the reason she was gone, was because she was married to him.

Jumping the fence, he went to the back door and bashed it in. Today, he didn't feel like concealing his entry. Going to the wall, he entered the disarm code for the security system. Two ferocious barks sounded from the living room, and the dog peeked around the corner. The abrupt manner in which he entered made the animal timid. Its tail wagged, but it was cautious to approach, sensing the commander's emotional turmoil.

He glanced in its direction. "Do you want out?"

The dog looked uncertainly at the ajar door, hanging askew from where the bolts warped the frame under the pressure. It cocked its head to the side and looked quizzically at Mercer. Then it padded over and sat at his feet, staring up at him with big brown eyes while its tail thumped a slow rhythm on the floor.

He stepped past the furry creature and conducted another thorough examination of Argus Yancy's cottage. The dog followed him from room to room. "Bugger." He hoped he'd find bomb-making materials or some indication of a payoff or payout. Maybe it was an unlucky coincidence Mercer had been followed to Yancy's secret watering hole.

Returning to the living room, he found a bottle of Irish whiskey in the liquor cabinet and filled a glass. He took a seat in Yancy's chair and turned on the man's laptop. The dog nudged his arm with its wet nose, so it could slide its head onto his thigh.

Absently, Mercer petted the dog while he went through Yancy's e-mails and internet history. When the dog grew bored, it went out the open back door to play in the yard.

Yancy wasn't on the dark web. There was no illicit activity, so to speak, but he did have a folder on his computer which contained several photos of the tavern and Lucie. Some of the shots were blurry. With the exception of a handful of selfies, the rest were candids. Mercer wasn't positive Lucie knew she was being photographed. Perhaps Yancy was a twisted fuck who liked to date women half his age or, more accurately, fantasize and clandestinely photograph women half his age, but nothing in Yancy's cottage indicated he had voyeuristic tendencies. Maybe he kept those things elsewhere.

A few deep barks sounded, and Mercer heard a car door. He put the laptop on the table and rested the gun in his lap, pointing it at the front entrance. The lights were off, but the computer provided some illumination.

"Cynthia?" Yancy called, unaware he wasn't alone. "Where are you?"

"Who the bloody hell is Cynthia?" Mercer asked. The copper reached for his weapon, but Mercer shook his head, aiming a little higher. "I wouldn't try it."

Yancy flipped on the light. "I know you."

"You should."

"What did you do with Cynthia?"

"Once again, I don't know who that is. Is she another woman you're stalking?"

"I'm not stalking anyone. She's my dog." Yancy let out a shrill whistle.

Mercer watched the way the man panicked before the spaniel pawed open the broken back door and charged at her owner. Yancy knelt down, hugging the creature as she lapped at his face. Mercer waited for the reunion to end before he spoke again.

"I'm not in the business of hurting innocents. That includes pets." He nodded at the couch, jerking his gun so the detective would take a seat. "I don't imagine you can say the same."

"What the bloody hell are you talking about?"

"Your signature is on the reports. You went to my house. You saw my wife. The things that sadist did to her. And you and your inspectors claim to never have a bloody clue how it happened. You tried to blame me, but that didn't work. Until recently, I thought the Met was nothing more than incompetent wankers. Now I suspect you're harboring a killer. You will tell me everything I want to know, or matters will become unpleasant."

"Your wife was murdered?"

Mercer's eye twitched. "Yes."

"Mercer?"

"Yes."

"Inspector Brickle told me about a discrepancy. Was that your wife's case?"

"Yes," Mercer spat. "You're in charge of the task force. It's your command. You control your men. You are ultimately responsible." He moved out of the chair and went to Yancy, removing the man's weapon. "Your notepad and one other were missing pages. What was removed?"

"Do you really think breaking into my house and threatening me is the way to go, mate?"

"I've tried everything else. You wouldn't see me. This time, you have no choice. I expect the truth."

"Bloody hell. There is no truth. We investigated. Whatever leads we had, we explored. You were our prime suspect. Shit, you were our only suspect."

"Lee Farnsworth's notepad was also missing pages,

and he's dead. What did he see?"

"Nothing." Some troubling thought went through Yancy's mind.

"That, right there." Mercer poked the gun in Yancy's direction for emphasis. "What was that?"

"What?"

Letting out a huff, Mercer shifted his aim to the dog. "Last chance."

"I don't know. That was quite some time ago. Do you have any idea how many scenes I visit in a week?"

"Stop deflecting. Answer the question."

Yancy climbed to his feet and stepped toward Mercer. "I am sorry your wife was killed. I don't know how it happened, and I don't know anything about these missing pages. But if you think you can break into my home, hold me at gunpoint, threaten my dog, and interrogate me, you have another think coming."

"Did you send someone to blow up my car?"

That comment froze Yancy in his tracks. Some other thought crossed his mind, and he raised his palms in surrender. "That's what this is about. Whoever murdered your wife is after you."

"I don't know."

"Isn't that why you're here?"

"I don't give a shit about my safety. I promised Michelle I'd find whoever hurt her. And until I do, I refuse to do anything else."

"Why did it take you so long to come looking?"

"I never stopped. I just didn't have any leads until now, and because of you, they are nothing but dead ends. One way or another, you will tell me what was removed from your notes."

"I can't remember."

"Convenient." Mercer shoved Yancy backward. "Get comfortable. You're not leaving until I get answers."

"Farnsworth's dead," Yancy said, as if the

statement were nothing more than the weather forecast. "His notes were missing, as are mine. My notes are a collection of statements made by my officers. When we reviewed the notebooks, the same information was missing from both pads. Am I correct in believing you've reviewed the files several times?"

"Yes."

"And so have some of your government contacts. You never noticed anything missing until now?"

"I was never given access to the notepads. Were you keeping them from me?"

"It wasn't me. It appears the Met is taking on water."

"Why should I believe you?"

"I don't give a shit what you believe." Yancy climbed off the couch and went into the kitchen.

"Careful," Mercer warned.

"It's Cynthia's dinnertime. I have to feed her." He poured some kibble into the bowl and gave the dog a quick pat. His gaze went to the broken back door. "The SAS didn't teach you how to enter a home quietly?"

"Be thankful I didn't use a grenade."

Yancy swallowed, finding that bit of news disconcerting. "Here's how I see it. Someone killed your wife. From what I recall, it looked like it was you. Presumably, the killer wanted to frame you. Perhaps he planned to end you after her. I see no reason to speculate as to motive. What's done is done, but cumulatively, isolated incidents since then are rather disconcerting. Farnsworth was killed in a fight a few weeks after your wife's murder. A couple of months after that, we were urged to back off the investigation by a government agency. The case was growing cold, and we were coming under political pressure. I assumed your mates pulled some strings to conceal your involvement. But if you really are innocent, someone on your end is responsible, and he's pitting you against the police force and fucking with anyone who gets in his way. Maybe that's why this nutter tried to permanently silence you last night. He wanted to put a permanent end to this investigation."

"Really?" Mercer asked skeptically.

"Fine. How do you read it?"

Parker's theory reverberated in Mercer's mind. The bloody Yank was right. "Let's say for a moment I believe that rubbish. I need proof."

"I can get you copies of the official requests, chain of custody forms, transfer of evidence receipts. Whatever you need. But you have to come to the office to get them."

"So you can arrest me?"

The brief bit of hope left Yancy's face. "I don't have the ability to access those materials outside the office. If you want them, you'll have to come with me to get them."

"No." Mercer checked the time. "Here are my terms. Tomorrow, you get copies of everything that proves you and the rest of your bloody task force aren't involved. I'll have a message sent to you with a location. You will drop the materials off alone. No trackers. No surveillance. If you disregard these terms or fail to comply, you will face the consequences. I know everything about you, Argus. And I know everything about your family, your three darling children, the ex-wife you aren't over, and Lucie's pub. You fuck with me, I'll fuck with them."

"You said you don't hurt innocents."

"I'm a man with nothing left. How far do you want to push me?"

"Anything else?"

"I need to know precisely where Inspector Brickle

was last night and who he's been speaking to these last few days."

"Why?"

"The why doesn't concern you. Do as I say, or the next time I pay you a visit, it won't be so civil."

NINE

"How do you know something isn't about to pop off?" Bastian asked.

"I don't." Mercer stared across the square at the pre-selected park bench.

The instructions were simple. Yancy was told to bring the documents to the bench at precisely noon where an envelope was taped beneath the seat so the copper could inconspicuously slide the documents inside. After that was done, Yancy was to vacate the park immediately. As soon as the coast was clear, Mercer would collect the documents and check for trackers. The envelope was Bastian's creation built out of a microfilament designed to shield electronic transmissions. Once the documents were deemed safe, Mercer would review them elsewhere.

"He's approaching from the west entrance." Mercer nodded in Yancy's direction as the detective walked briskly down the path and took an uncertain seat on the bench. "Does he look nervous?"

"A bit." Bastian glanced at his tablet, which was

monitoring the area for radio frequencies. Yancy didn't appear to be in contact with any of his comrades, but if the police were using cell phones instead of radios, it would be nearly impossible to tell. Implementing a jammer in a crowded park could prevent that, but it might warrant unwanted attention. "He looks worried. Undoubtedly, a side effect of you threatening his family."

Mercer shrugged.

"Do you think he knows you were bluffing?"

"Was I?"

"Pish."

Mercer watched Yancy get up from the bench and walk away. "I haven't spotted any other bobbies."

Bastian put the tablet down. "I'm not getting anything, Jules. It should be clear to make the pick-up." Bastian stood. "And for the record, you're being bloody ridiculous. That information could have been collected in a civilized, professional manner. Instead, you're acting like an unhinged hoodlum. You're making these problems worse. You might need police assistance to deal with the bomber, but instead, you alienated the only help we're liable to get."

"I'm not convinced one of the bobbies isn't the bomber. And we both know Yancy wouldn't have handed over the information if I asked politely. He wouldn't even grant me an audience. I had no choice but to force his compliance."

"What did he say about the missing notes?"

"He doesn't remember what they contained, but he believes someone higher up the food chain removed them."

"What did Brickle say?"

"Brickle had no explanation for the missing pages, but he appeared as confounded as I was. I doubt answers will be forthcoming. You can't honestly believe the entire lot isn't rotten. They left me no choice. I did what I had to."

"You did what you wanted, like always."

As Bastian crossed the square, he remained facing forward. He didn't look around. He didn't make his intentions apparent. He was performing a task, and in the event the police were monitoring the area, they wouldn't realize what was happening until the documents were in hand.

Mercer remained hidden. His eyes darted this way and that, scanning for danger or hints of a trap. And then he felt it, the tingling twinge of being observed. He searched for the source. The park was crowded. Too crowded. It could be anyone. The adrenaline surged, and his heart rate kicked up a few notches. Inhaling, he forced everything around him to quiet. He needed to focus.

As he searched the greenery and open expanse, his brain eliminated everyone who didn't pose a threat. His heightened acuity paused on a figure beneath a large tree. The man was partially concealed by the trunk and sweeping branches. But the moment he noticed Mercer watching him, he tucked a phone into his pocket and abandoned his position. Setting off at a brisk pace, the unsub crossed back onto the paved path and headed for one of the exits.

Mercer raced after him, pushing his way through a group of joggers. He would not let his target escape again. Whoever this bastard was, he already interfered one too many times. And if he thought he could blow Mercer to bits, he had another think coming.

Catching a glimpse of a dark coat moving a few meters ahead, Mercer broke into a run. Before his target was within reach, a troupe of children entered the park. It must have been a school trip because hordes of kids and harried looking teachers poured out of the parked buses. Mercer tried to maneuver around them, dodging to the left. He was stuck at the main gate, forced to the side as the crowd took up the entire exit.

The concrete walls surrounding the gate were too high to climb over. There was only one way out, and it was through the gate. Mercer scrambled to find an opening. Anything that would put him closer to his target, but the man was too far ahead. The target made it out of the gate in the nick of time, before the entrance became impassible. His dark coat disappeared around the corner and out of sight.

"Bloody hell." Mercer spun in place and raced toward Bastian. "Bas, we have to go. Now."

Confused, Bastian scanned the area. He didn't spot anyone from law enforcement. "It's okay." He held up the RF scanner. "The documents are clean. No sign of a tracker."

"The bomber was here." Mercer pointed emphatically at the tree. "The bastard was right there. I lost him in the crowd. He went out the exit. We need to head him off." Breaking into a sprint, he led the way to the next nearest exit which let out on a perpendicular boulevard. "He's wearing a dark coat."

"I'll try to tap into the CCTV. At least there are cameras everywhere. If I get eyes on him, I'll let you know."

Mercer turned down the street. His target had too great of a lead, but he knew the man had voyeuristic tendencies. Assuming the son of a bitch believed he bested Mercer and escaped, he might double back to observe what the former SAS commander planned to do. At least, that's what Mercer was counting on.

As he ran down the street, hating having to loop around the long way, he couldn't shake the thought Yancy tipped off the bomber. It was the only thing that made any sense. Ever since the explosion, Mercer had taken extreme care to prevent anyone from monitoring him. When this was over, he would have another chat with the detective, and this time, it wouldn't be so pleasant.

As he approached the park entrance from the outside, the buses pulled away. The sidewalk remained congested, but it was no longer gridlocked. Stopping, Mercer surveyed the area. When he spotted a dark coat several meters ahead, he pushed through the crowd, moving quickly through the throng until he grabbed the man by the scruff of his neck.

Throwing up an arm, the man spun. He hadn't shaved in weeks. The rest of his clothing was tattered and dirty. "Oi, unhand me."

Mercer stared at him for a long moment. "Where'd you find the coat? Who gave it to you?"

"It's mine. Some fellow tossed it into the refuse bin. A nice coat like this." He stroked the lapel and narrowed his eyes. "I saw it first. You get your own."

Dropping his hold on the man, Mercer let out an exasperated huff. "I don't want the bleeding coat. Where did the man go? What did he look like?"

"Looked about like you. Maybe a little taller. His hair was a smidge lighter. Is he your brother?"

Mercer wanted to shake the answers out of this guy. "Which way was he traveling?"

The guy looked around and pointed across the street. "He went that way."

Moving swiftly through the crosswalk, Mercer studied his surroundings. Without knowing what the target was now wearing, he couldn't continue pursuit. So he waited. Maybe the hunted would decide to resume his role as the hunter.

After circling the area for fifteen minutes, Mercer's phone buzzed. "Jules," Bastian said, "did you find him?"

"Negative."

"I'm patched into the surveillance feed, but I can't access the recorded footage remotely. I've seen several men with dark coats."

"Disregard. He tossed the coat. Let's regroup. We'll discuss these matters in person."

The pair reconvened at the train station. They waited separately on the platform. Each vigilant to monitor the area, but since it wasn't peak hours, not many people crowded around them. When the train came, they entered and went to the rear of the car.

Once Mercer was certain none of the passengers posed a danger, he spoke in a hushed tone. "The bomber must be working with Yancy."

"How did you spot him? Did you recognize him? The bomber, not the detective."

"I never saw his face. I barely caught a glimpse of him." Mercer looked out the window. "I felt him."

"Those are some bloody fantastic instincts, mate. Just like that time in Kandahar."

Mercer's eyes blazed. "Not exactly. We stopped that son of a bitch. We have yet to identify this one." He told Bastian about his exchange with the homeless man. "Our target is trained. He may be police or military. He knows how to place a charge, and he's excellent at stealth tracking. He also knows how to change his appearance and disappear. He can blend into his environment." Mercer's lip twitched. "Bugger. Parker's right. It's like he's one of us."

"How do you think he happened upon us this afternoon?"

"Yancy."

"First, Brickle. Now, Yancy. Do you think he's working for the police? Or the police are working for him?"

"I don't know." Mercer reached for the documents and read them carefully. As promised, Yancy provided the internal memorandums showing what evidence was logged, what reports were made, and who checked the materials out. He also provided Brickle's call sheet for last night. The inspector worked late and was responding to a domestic dispute in North London at the same time Mercer was being stalked. On the surface, it appeared everything the copper said was true, but paperwork could be doctored easily enough. Mercer tucked the pages safely into his jacket for a more thorough review later.

"What's our plan, Jules?"

"We split up. When I know more, I'll be in contact."

"That's lunacy. If the man you chased out of the park was the bomber from last night, he's getting ballsy. He must be planning another strike. You need back-up."

"I need you safe."

"Jules, have you forgotten we've been in worse scrapes. We function best as a team. You're being suicidal."

"I'm being pragmatic. Stay vigilant. Until we know how the bomber is tracking us, we need to take extreme care. We're running dark until this is over. Is that understood?"

"I suppose."

"And keep your distance from Hans and Donovan. They're sitting ducks. We don't want to draw this bastard's attention to them."

"It's already too late. If he's been watching you, he's seen us. He knows about us. And for the record, those ducks have pinpoint accuracy and plenty of firepower. It could serve in our favor."

"Now who's being daft? Compile the intel. As soon as we identify this bastard, we'll go on the offensive.

Until then, we disappear." The train came to a stop, and Mercer went to the door. He had a lot to think about.

TEN

Mercer glanced around the tiny hovel. He answered several adverts and rented four different places, each under a different alias. Despite the extra measures, he didn't believe any of them were secure. He kept his belongings tidy and compact so they could be moved at a moment's notice. He also refused to stay in any one location for more than a day for fear this bastard would figure out some way of tracking him.

The intel Yancy provided was on par with what he promised. Michelle's murder might have been covered up by someone much higher in the government, perhaps even one of the clandestine agencies for which Mercer and his team performed missions. The only way to know anything for certain was to speak to Yancy again. However, the bobby wasn't taking any chances either.

Patrol units were positioned outside the DCI's cottage. It would be nearly impossible to sneak past them. Plus, the barking dog would alert the cops of an intruder instantly. Instead, Mercer would have to find another way to corner Yancy. He knew the detective's habits. So he'd have to wait him out.

Unfortunately, Mercer had shown his hand when he threatened Yancy's family. That was a mistake he regretted, but he could do nothing to change it now. And going to the police station was asking for trouble. Bastian was right. Mercer shouldn't have acted so rashly. He needed the copper's help, and if he couldn't track down Yancy, he would have no choice but to go to the station and hope he wouldn't be imprisoned or worse. With the bomber on the loose, being locked up would make him an easy target. And that was not an option.

Brickle appeared to be uninvolved in the evidence tampering and the bombing, but Mercer wasn't convinced. He flipped through the dossier. Brickle was a loner. His life was the job. He didn't have a family or any nasty habits, so until Mercer found a pressure point, he would stay clear of the inspector. Frankly, Brickle was too low on the totem pole to provide the type of intel and resources the bomber needed to continue pursuit. But Mercer couldn't shake the feeling the bomber used Brickle to obtain his phone number. And that meant trouble. Maybe the London police really did have a leak.

While he considered methods of cornering Yancy without undue interference, his mind kept returning to the bomber. He had a vague description of the man. Tall, light to medium brown hair, and athletically built. At least that's how the homeless man described him. Those details fit dozens of men he had encountered over the years.

The bomber was trained in explosives and methods of tracking. He must have been a soldier, familiar with London and Mercer. But was that from reading a profile or a personal encounter? How much information did the police possess on their number one suspect?

Only Yancy could answer that question, so Mercer went back to devising a plan for their next rendezvous. His best bet was Lucie's Tavern. The downside was the bomber had tracked him there. If the bomber were to pick up Mercer's trail again, this would be the place to do it.

Every night for a week, Mercer went to Lucie's to wait for Yancy. He changed his mode of transportation every time. Sometimes, he'd walk. Other times, he used public transportation. Occasionally, he'd get a rideshare or taxi. As of yet, the detective hadn't made an appearance. Perhaps Yancy was just as leery of being followed and monitored, or one of the blokes at the tavern alerted Yancy of Mercer's presence and told him to stay away.

While Mercer made the trek for the sixth time, he reached one undeniable truth. The man who murdered Michelle was connected to the man who planted the bomb. And that man was trained, lethal, and knew him intimately.

Alex Parker told him as much on the phone. He heard her words, knew they had meaning and value, but until the afternoon in the park, during his second encounter with the bomber, he had trouble wrapping his mind around it. Now Bastian was tasked with going through the service records and files of every man Mercer worked with on the off chance one of them was the bomber or killer. That was a long list, full of highly capable and deadly men. Any one of them could be to blame. The copper had to know who the bomber was. It was the only logical way the bomber knew to show up at the park and maybe even the pub. If Yancy didn't show tonight, Mercer would risk imprisonment for the chance to speak to him. This couldn't go on. He had a killer to find and a bomber to stop.

Taking his usual seat at the corner of the bar, he waited for Lucie to fill his glass. It had become their ritual, just like the wary looks she tossed in his direction. She made it clear on his second visit she was not a fan of his presence, but he earned his keep. She poured the single malt and pushed it in front of him.

The night droned on. Argus Yancy didn't stop by. A few hours later, Mercer intervened when one of the addicts became loud and belligerent. The tavern was usually mellow, but the underlying current of tension was palpable tonight. One misstep would lead to a brawl, and Mercer didn't want anyone to ring the police. For all he knew, he was wanted for breaking into Yancy's house and extorting the detective.

"Thanks," Lucie said when he returned to his seat. "That's the third time you've gotten rid of some tossers this week. You keep it up and I'll have to put you on the payroll. So cut it out. I can't afford to hire anyone else."

"I'm not looking for compensation."

"What are you looking for?"

He didn't speak, finding the contents of the glass particularly satisfying after the brief physical altercation. It was like turning a valve and releasing the pressure, making the day-to-day slightly more bearable. Having to be patient and wait for Yancy was taking a toll. Mercer was a man of action. He found the waiting insufferable. "Do you know a man named Argus?"

"Why?"

"He told me about this tavern, but I've never seen him here."

She turned her hips in preparation for retreat. "Maybe you have the wrong place."

For the rest of the night, he kept an eye on her, but she never made a move for the phone to tip off Yancy. Unaware of what Yancy's precise connection to this tavern was, Mercer assumed the detective might be a recreational drug user who wanted to go somewhere off the beaten path to hide his dirty little habit. Or he and the tavern owner had an affair which recently ended. Regardless of the reason, he needed to speak to Yancy. He couldn't take many more nights like this. Eventually, the bomber would surface, and no one would be safe.

Even after last call, Mercer remained seated. The trek back to the rental held little appeal. He finished his drink, craving the oblivion it could provide. He was exhausted. He couldn't remember the last time he slept for more than a four hour stretch, and it was even longer since he had a nightmare free rest.

As the other patrons filed out, he eyed the bottles behind the counter. The liquor stores closed hours earlier. Not to mention, getting piss while being stalked by an unknown assailant wasn't practical. He should leave, so he could start the monotony fresh in a few hours. But he didn't move off the stool.

"Do you have someplace to go?" Lucie asked.

"No."

Nodding, she bid the other bartender good night and locked the door. "Why do you want to speak to Argus?"

"That's none of your concern."

She grabbed a glass and the bottle of single malt and sat down beside him. "This is my place. That makes it my concern." She poured one for herself and refilled his. "You know how this works, Julian. If you expect anything from me, you need to give me something."

"He works for the Metropolitan police."

"I'm aware."

That affirmation surprised Mercer. "Okay."

She gulped down a mouthful. "Okay? What the bloody hell does that mean? You have yet to tell me why you want to speak to him."

"Why do you care?"

"You're a formidable man. Do you work for the Met?"

The look of disgust was obvious.

"Military?" she asked.

"Former."

Lucie cocked her head to the side, taking a smaller sip and studying him over the rim. "What do you do now?"

"I'm a security specialist."

"Whatever the bloody hell that means." She finished her drink and poured another splash into her glass. "Does that have anything to do with your obsession with Argus?"

"No."

"Bugger." She stared him in the eye. "Why do you want to talk to him?"

Realizing this conversation wasn't going anywhere, he emptied the contents of his glass, ignoring the burn at the back of his throat. "I should go."

"Is it really that terrible?"

Unsure what possessed him to respond, he said, "I believe he knows who killed my wife."

"Shit." Lucie finished her drink and poured another one for him. "I'm sorry, mate." She brushed her hair out of her face and went behind the bar. Picking up a tiny calendar, she flipped the pages. "Have you tried speaking to him at work?"

"Getting in to see him is complicated."

"Sure." She nodded as if that made sense. "He should be dropping by either tomorrow or the next day. I don't imagine there will be any trouble."

"I just want to talk." Depending on how Yancy responded would determine what sort of trouble ensued.

Lucie put her hand on his forearm. It was a gesture that instantly made him uncomfortable. "I'm a great bullshit detector. It's my super power. I picked it up after years of listening to drunks ramble incessantly. So if it turns out you're lying to me, I'm going to be raging mad. But something tells me you're a good man. Just lost. Argus will help you."

Mercer moved to stand, but Lucie refilled his glass. "Thanks," he said.

"Lock up, all right?"

"Leave it," Mercer said.

She put the bottle down, brushed her hand over his, and went up the back staircase.

Lifting the glass, he took a sip. The room wobbled, and he rubbed his eyes. His body was too stubborn to blackout. He took another drink and leaned back, his gaze bouncing around the darkened room. Staying was stupid. She could be playing him. Right now, she could be upstairs calling Yancy or the police to pick him up. She could even be phoning the bomber. After all, the bastard did plant the explosive only a couple of meters from here. And Mercer didn't know anything about her or her connection to Yancy, but he was tired. If someone were to show up, at least then he might get some answers. Truthfully, he was itching for a fight, and he was drunk enough to believe a showdown could solve everything.

This was a quiet tavern on a small side street in the east end of London. Lucie's flat was above. She lived and worked here. She said she didn't want trouble, so Mercer chose to believe her. But his presence night after night was inviting trouble. She just didn't know it yet.

He moved from the bar to one of the booths and settled into the ancient upholstery, letting his eyes close. The images his brain conjured were worse when he was inebriated. Flashes of wars he fought and enemies he killed went through his mind. But those weren't nearly as troubling as remembering the final moments he spent holding his wife. She was murdered twenty kilometers from here in the house they shared. A thought went through his mind. He needed to go home. The solution was there.

Licking his lips, he reached for the glass and drained the contents. He couldn't deal with that now. He needed a few hours to get his mind right. He needed a break. But only on a few rare occasions did his mind slow long enough to give him peace. He'd get there. Tonight, he'd get there. The nearly empty bottle would bring about additional torment, but inevitably, it would lead to nothingness for a few short hours. The break from the nightmares would be welcome, and if the cops or the bomber arrived, he'd deal with them.

The warmth spread through his belly. Idly, he wondered how many more nights he would spend in the pub. At first, Lucie was cautious of his presence, but he never caused trouble and kept to himself. In the last week, he became a fixture. He always paid his tab, tossing in extra to cover any inconvenience his presence caused, and dealt with the tossers and plonkers who threatened to trash the place with their pathetic arguments and swinging fists. This pub was his port in the storm while he waited for the lightning bolt to strike. Perhaps tonight would be the night. If not, Lucie promised it would happen in the next two days. Even if he didn't trust her enough to believe her, her promise that Yancy would show up was enough to keep him from walking through the doors of the police station and facing unknown consequences.

The world slowed in the deafening silence. Thoughts flickered and stopped. For the next few hours, Julian Mercer slept in the back booth of the tavern.

Something creaked, and he shot up straight. The brightness of morning burned through his retinas and set his skull on fire. Without a thought, he lifted his Sig Sauer from the table and pointed it at the front door. No one was there. He was alone. A glance at his watch told him it was time to go.

Pouring the remainder of the bottle into his glass, he drank, starting his morning with the hair of the dog. It was impossible to be hungover if he avoided sobriety, he reasoned. Then he put the empty glass and bottle on top of the bar with a few quid. Slipping out into the early morning light, he donned a pair of sunglasses and surveyed the commuters.

A dark sedan pulled away from the curb as he crossed the street. He narrowed his eyes, but the windows were tinted and he couldn't see the driver. But he'd seen the car several times before. He watched it turn and disappear from sight.

Wary, he took a different route to collect his belongings before relocating to a new flat. He watched the pedestrians and traffic patterns like they might be concealing insurgents. By the time he made it to the second location, his focus was on his pounding head and upset stomach and not his paranoid delusions.

Grabbing a new burner phone, he dialed Bastian. "Any progress?"

"I'm clearing names from the list as we speak. None of our known enemies is operating in the area, so I don't think the bomber is a kidnapper we faced. I reviewed the surveillance footage from the night of the explosion and that afternoon at the park. The man doesn't move like any police officer I've ever seen. He moves like an operative."

"I agree." Mercer's thoughts went to the government oversight concerning his wife's murder. Yancy insisted some higher-up tampered with the evidence. Could the killer be one of their military contacts? Was he the same person now gunning for him?

Reading Mercer's mind, Bastian said, "Parker believes the bomber and killer might be one and the same, but even if they aren't, I think they're working together."

"What about the police connection?"

"The paperwork indicates otherwise, so I'm creating a new list of potential suspects based solely on your military connections. The bomber knows you, Jules. Based on Parker's findings, Michelle's killer did too. So anyone who was serving a tour when Michelle was murdered or at the present is being removed. We'll narrow it from there. How's it coming on your end?"

"I've been told Yancy will show in the next day or two. After that, I'm going home."

ELEVEN

"Bugger." Mercer slammed his fist on the table. How many times did he and Bastian read through these news articles? He never saw a pattern. The only commonality was the nature of the crime–homicides. Of course, what drew the newsman's attention was the similarities of the victims in regards to Mercer's own tragedy. Those slaughtered were related to military and government officials.

Bastian fleshed it out and didn't find a connection. Even Mercer, in all his conspiracy theory glory, failed to find a common thread, but Alexis Parker insisted she spotted one. She noticed the discrepancies in the reports and the crime scene. She made it clear she had no qualms when it came to pointing out the cold hard truth, and Mercer needed her icy logic.

He rubbed his eyes and dug through the files again. The murders occurred throughout the United Kingdom. The method of killing was different each time. The victims didn't know each other. The families weren't connected. The survivors, men like him, served in different military branches with no overlap as to missions. Like Bastian surmised, the survivors never met prior to their personal tragedies and never crossed paths afterward. Most were forced to resign or retire. Only a handful remained in the field, and those who did met untimely deaths.

If the newsman was correct in his assertion, the same party was responsible for all these murders. While the motive wasn't clear, the result was. Those who worked in special units and intelligence were targeted and removed. The few stable enough to continue to fulfill their duties were killed in action or in a freak accident. Someone was orchestrating this, but Mercer couldn't decide if it was a rogue operative acting alone or an operative acting on behalf of another party.

Before the debacle at Yancy's home, Donovan had the police look into these other killings. Inspector Brickle was checking to see if any of them experienced evidence tampering, but as of yet, Mercer didn't know. From the files he and his team reviewed, nothing stood out. Bastian forwarded the details to Alex, but since Mercer abandoned his phone several times, the only way the American could make contact was through an online dropbox. However, she was following his instructions and waiting for him to reach out.

Get out of your bloody head, Mercer's inner voice snarled. He needed help. After picking up the phone, he dialed Parker. When her voice came over the line, it sounded strange. Mercer looked at the clock, realizing the time difference.

"What have you found?" he asked, not bothering to waste time with a greeting or apology.

She let out a tired groan. "Shit."

"Brilliant," he replied. "Why am I wasting my

time?"

Her voice went hard as nails. "If you hang up on me again, don't call back." The sound of paper rustling came over the line, followed by the clicking of a mouse. "Carlton Rhoade is a piece of work. However, his research looks legit. I've done some digging, and I had my friends at the OIO do the same. The son of a bitch is definitely on to something."

"What?"

"I'm not sure. I looked through the files Bastian sent. On the surface, they appear entirely unrelated."

"I know."

"Here's the thing. Each victim was killed with a weapon identical to one kept on the premises. With the exception of Rourke's case in which ballistics matched the gun used to a firearm registered to a MI5 agent, the killer always made sure to bring an identical weapon. He must have known what was on hand. That's the commonality. That's what indicates these murders were committed by the same person."

"Like the knife he used on Michelle." Mercer blew out a slow breath. "So he might not be someone I know."

"Actually, I was thinking the opposite."

"I don't understand."

"It's someone with a connection to all the victims." She paused, but Mercer didn't rush to fill the space. He wanted to hear what else she had to say. "That one abnormality, the Rourke case, might be an outlier, a mistake by Rhoade who grouped that crime with the rest, or the killer got sloppy. I'm still working on that, but in the meantime, I've been trying to figure out the connection between you and the other victims."

"What about the police reports?"

"Nothing out of the ordinary. DCI Yancy is in charge of a special homicide task force which oversaw all the crime scenes. Based on the paperwork, it sounds like the task force was specifically designed to deal with violent crimes involving military and government personnel. The intel and investigation on these cases was shared with a similar team at MI5. The London police may not be responsible for the evidence tampering."

"When was the task force formed?"

"Hang on." She keyed something into the computer. "I don't know. Yancy's task force was already in place when the first of these homicides occurred, which leads me to believe there are more killings we don't know about."

"Michelle wasn't the first?"

"No."

"Bloody hell." If he had known ahead of time some psycho was out there, he would have taken measures to keep her protected. He should have known. He should have saved her. "We need the police records. We need MI5's records. We need to know how many there have been."

"I agree."

"Well?"

"I can't get that information. My colleagues can't either. Bastian and Donovan have collected several police files, but if my theory is correct, you're also getting the runaround. Someone on your side of the pond wants to keep a lid on this. They don't want anyone to know what's going on, that includes you and your team."

"Yancy," Mercer hissed.

"I don't know. I finished running backgrounds on him and Inspector Brickle. Nothing popped. If they are covering up these crimes, so is every member of the task force."

"Except one."

"Who?" she asked.

"Lee Farnsworth. Someone silenced him before he could talk."

"Maybe. All I can say is this is a lot bigger than you thought. Your best bet is to work with New Scotland Yard and MI5, at least until you gain access to the intel you want. You have connections and contacts. Someone's bound to be straight with you. You just have to find a reliable source. It sounds like..."

"What?" Mercer prodded.

"A serial killer or a terrorist plot. I've seen it happen. One of your special forces guys might have gone off the reservation."

"You sound like a nutter."

"I learned from the best."

He smirked, despite himself. "This ought to be interesting."

"I'm no behaviorist, but based on the varied methods of killing and the frequency of the kills, whoever this guy is, he's been trained. Either he always had a taste for it or he got a taste while serving and he liked it. I haven't figured out how or why he picks his victims. I don't know why he killed your wife, but I won't stop looking until I have answers. I promise you that."

Mercer stared out the window. "He has experience with explosives."

"Anything else?"

He thought for a moment, recalling the scattered details the man with the coat provided. "If he was an agent or in the military, we should have been able to identify him on the surveillance footage. He would have been in a database. The bastard knows how to avoid being seen or how to alter footage."

"Sounds like special ops."

"Or he's a bloody ghost."

"You're thinking spy?"

"Perhaps." He leafed through the pages again. "Or his identity's been scrubbed, or he has a team in play. Keep looking for a connection. When you have his name, I want it immediately. Drop whatever progress you make into that online box. Bas is monitoring it."

"Sure. Be careful, Mercer."

That sentiment was pointless. He would exercise just enough care to hunt down the hunter. Then he would make the man pay. What happened afterward was irrelevant. He had one goal. And after speaking to Parker, he was another step closer.

TWELVE

If Julian Mercer spent one more moment in the shitty hovel he rented, he'd go screaming mad. Ever since he spoke to Parker, he'd done nothing but review the intel. Whoever this sick, twisted prick was, he murdered Michelle, took countless other lives, and didn't plan to stop anytime soon. The killer was someone with special training and incredible skills. No wonder it had taken Mercer and his team so long to find a solid lead. The killer was one of their own. He wasn't a random psycho off the street, like the police insisted. Michelle's murder was a perfectly timed and expertly conducted hit.

Locking up, Mercer walked briskly down the path. He scanned the streets for signs of danger, convinced his wife's killer was also his yet-to-be-identified stalker. For some reason, the killer set his sights on Mercer, and that was a fatal mistake. Mercer would make sure of it.

As soon as he was positive he wasn't being followed, he stopped by the rented flat to check for messages. Perhaps the bomber had phoned again. He examined the doorjamb but didn't find any tripwires. After that, he swept the flat, which his team emptied and wiped. The only signs that they had been there were the cell phones they left inside the locked cabinet.

Picking one up, he saw he had a missed call from the London police. Hitting another button, Mercer listened to the voicemail.

"Mr. Mercer, this is Inspector Brickle. I have some news. We should speak in person. Call me back."

Even though Mercer never intended on waltzing into the police station, he wanted to hear what Brickle had to say. Information on his wife's killer was his kryptonite, so he left the flat and headed to the Met. He wanted to speak to Yancy and Brickle, but he didn't know if he could trust either one. And now that he was aware of the task force, he was on the fence about the role the police played in investigating Michelle's murder.

In truth, Mercer fit the killer's profile, but so did each of the other targets. The authorities should have realized Mercer wasn't to blame. They should have disclosed what they knew. Perhaps a few tragedies could have been avoided, and Mercer would have been able to home in on the hunter before he became the hunted.

Deciding to throw caution to the wind, he entered the police station and asked to speak to Yancy or Brickle. As predicted, the DCI was in a meeting across town and couldn't be disturbed. But Inspector Brickle was available.

Mercer gave the desk sergeant his name and took a seat, wondering if this was a ploy to lure him to the station so he could be arrested. The police knew about the break-in since units were monitoring Yancy's neighborhood. But to Mercer's surprise, he wasn't handcuffed. Instead, Inspector Brickle came to fetch him from the front desk.

"I wondered when I'd see you again." Brickle glanced around. "On second thought, let's have a chat in private, shall we?" He jerked his head to a darkened room off to the side.

"Is this an interrogation?" Mercer eyed the table and two-way mirror.

"Should it be?"

Mercer glared.

"Right, so after you left the other day, another chap dropped by. He asked that I check into possible evidence tampering in several other cases. Do you know what we found?"

"Not a bloody thing."

"Ah, I see you're clairvoyant." The inspector dropped into one of the chairs. "Those cases, just like your wife's, were reviewed by our colleagues in military intelligence. Something about that struck me oddly. They've been monitoring our progress on several homicides as of late. Care to explain why?"

"How would I know?"

"I guess you wouldn't." Brickle leaned back in the chair. "So what brings you by today?"

"I got your message."

"Right. You sure you don't want to confess to anything?"

"I didn't kill my wife."

For the first time since Mercer crossed paths with Brickle, the inspector seemed to believe him. "All right."

"Have you determined what was removed from the notepads?"

Brickle shook his head. "Our personal notes aren't recorded anywhere else. They are used to assist in writing our reports. We keep them on hand in case of discrepancies or to refresh ourselves before court. As far as we can tell, no one's looked at them since the day they were written."

"Bollocks." Mercer folded his arms over his chest, hoping to calm his desire to hit something. "There are records of the files being moved. You said military intelligence reviewed them. I need specifics. I need a name."

"Chain of custody forms aren't helpful. An agent signed out the evidence and logged it back in. We don't know who else had access when the intel was off the premises."

"Give me the agent's name."

"You don't want it."

"Stop playing games."

Before Brickle could respond, a uniformed officer knocked on the door. "Inspector, there's been another one." He glanced uncertainly at Mercer. "I didn't mean to interrupt, sir."

"No worries." In an instant, Brickle was out of his seat. "Do we have confirmation yet?"

"It hasn't detonated," the other cop responded.

"Where?" Mercer asked.

The copper glanced at him. "Hyde Park."

"Shit," Mercer swore. That's where he instructed Yancy to make the drop.

He marched out of the police station without another word. He had to get to the park. Sirens blared as units responded to the threat. Mercer stopped to consider the fastest route. Luckily, he spotted a taxicab on the corner. It was out-of-service, but he didn't care. He went up to the car and opened the door.

"Sorry, mate," the driver said.

Mercer slid into the seat and slammed the door. "Hyde Park." One of the bomb disposal units raced past. "Now." The driver looked as if he were about to protest. "I'll pay whatever you want. Just drive." Mercer saw the hesitation on the man's face and removed his firearm. "I won't say it again."

"Right away." The driver turned the key and zipped into traffic. London cabbies were required to have routes memorized and know their way around roadblocks, gridlock, and congested streets. The car pulled to a stop a few blocks from the park. The authorities had cordoned off the area. "This is as far as I go."

After tossing a hefty stack of bills into the front seat, Mercer stepped out of the cab and looked around. He could feel the electricity in the air. Reaching for his phone, he dialed Bastian and updated the analyst on the situation. "We need a visual. Find him. He must be here."

"Jules, we're looking for a needle in a haystack," Bastian protested as he attempted to remotely hack into the city's cameras. "Are you certain this nutter is the same one who tried to blow you up?"

"It has to be."

Evacuation protocols were in place. Uniformed police personnel waved visitors out of the main gates. The nearby Tube entrances were shut down while the underground railway was checked for devices and threats. If Mercer's suspicions were correct, the device would be planted at the park bench or inside the small pavilion where he and Bastian had waited.

Edging closer to the entrance, he stood on his tiptoes to catch a glimpse of the park over the crowd. The police cleared everyone out. As the last few people filed out, an elderly lady tripped and fell. The nearby officers went to assist, fearing the woman might be trampled. Mercer used the distraction to sneak past them.

He strode purposefully toward the drop-off location. As he drew closer, he spotted the bomb disposal unit. *I knew it*, he thought. From this distance, he couldn't see much, but the device appeared to be of a similar size to the one planted beneath his car. The experts would have to determine if it was made by the same man, but he was confident it was.

He spun, searching for the target. This hunter–killer, bomber, stalker, whatever he was–had to be close. Scanning the immediate vicinity, the only individuals in sight were the authorities. But since the bomber was trained, he could have infiltrated the group, disguised as one of their own. So Mercer waited, knowing the bomber would find him.

When two uniformed men with assault rifles took notice and approached, he decided it was time to go. He headed for the exit at a brisk pace, not too fast to warrant unwanted attention but fast enough to put a reasonable distance between him and the authorities. The last thing he needed was to be labeled a terrorist.

After he made it past the front gate, he nodded at the officers stationed there. The men following him did not continue pursuit. As far as any of them knew, Mercer was a straggler who took his time to vacate. As he continued down the sidewalk, he checked his phone to find it had no signal. Cell jammers were being used to prevent a remote detonation.

"Brilliant." Mercer crossed the street and headed away from the jammers. Then he phoned Bastian to see if there was any news.

Bastian tapped on his tablet a few times. The analyst searched for a news story to explain the situation, but nothing hit the wire yet. He stuck an earpiece in his ear and punched a few more buttons. "The police aren't using radio communication. We would hear chatter. The device must have a remote detonator."

"The bomber must be close. Anything on the camera feeds? Does anyone look suspicious?"

"Just you. To be honest, a lot of the feeds are fuzzy. The jammer is interfering with the signal, or the bomber is plugged into the feeds." Bastian clicked a few more keys. "Jules, why would he target the park? We already made the pick-up. It doesn't make sense."

"Nothing this bastard does makes sense. He wants to draw me out. He knew I'd hear about this, recognize his work, and show up."

"Then why the bloody hell are you there? It's a trap. And if it isn't, it could be another attempt to pin a crime on you. We scouted the area a couple of days ago. We have the ability and know-how to create one of these devices. Your car exploding could have been an accidental detonation. Circumstances point to us."

"And you say I'm paranoid."

"It's catching," Bas responded. "I'm on my way."

"No. I will handle this alone." Disconnecting, Mercer took a deep breath. Where would he go to flush out the enemy?

Before making it more than a few meters, he heard a loud pop, followed by a plume of smoke and the acrid smell of something burning. He sprinted back the way he came. Either the police detonated the device or the bomber did.

Several first responders streamed out of the park entrance. Sirens filled the air, and the number of law enforcement vehicles increased tenfold. Mercer watched as more people evacuated and nonessential personnel were removed from the area. Miraculously, no one appeared seriously injured, but the table at which he and Bastian sat days before was now nothing but a pile of broken, crumbling concrete slabs. At least its sturdy construction limited the blast radius. Some police officers were establishing a perimeter while others pushed the gawkers back.

Movement to the right caught Mercer's eye, and he spotted someone walking away. That had to be the bomber. The man was too calm, his attention focused on the ground in front of him and not the explosion or the chaos around him. No one behaved that way. It went against human nature.

Pushing through the crowds, Mercer lost sight of the man. Hurrying, he made it past the spectators and spotted the man turning a corner. Mercer gave chase, and the bomber broke into a run.

Pulling his weapon, Mercer slowed long enough to aim. He fired, but the bomber dove to the right. The bullet missed and hit the brick wall above the man's head. The bomber darted across the street. Mercer fired again. The second shot made contact, but it was nothing more than an inconvenient graze.

Mercer came to a dead stop, holding his aim steady. The screech of tires and the blaring of a car horn barely registered. Just as he fired, a car knocked him to the ground, and his perfect shot went high, impacting against a street sign.

Mercer swore, pulling himself to his feet. His gaze remained on the spot where the bomber disappeared. "Fuck." He slammed his palm against the car's bonnet.

The driver stepped out. "Are you all right?" Noticing the gun in Mercer's hand, he stepped back and held up his palms. A few cars behind him started honking, which drew the attention of the nearby authorities.

Someone shouted, "He has a gun."

Two nearby bobbies came closer to investigate. They were basic patrol, meant to keep the civilians away from the blast zone. "Sir, stop right there," one of them insisted.

Mercer turned, considering his chances of escape, but two more uniformed officers stepped in front of him. For the briefest moment, he considered fighting his way past them. But these new officers meant business. They were fully armed and wearing tactical gear. The explosion meant they were ready to wage war.

"Stay there," the closest one ordered.

Mercer raised his hands and got on his knees. "The man responsible is getting away." He jerked his head in the direction the bomber had gone. "He detonated the explosive and is escaping."

"How do you know that?"

"I just bloody do."

They searched Mercer, removing his weapon and cell phone. As they rifled through his wallet, Bastian arrived. Mercer cast a glance at his second-in-command, who stepped forward with credentials and a business card in hand. While the analyst spoke to the police, Mercer remained docile, processing everything he had learned in the last few days until he reached the only feasible conclusion. The bomber knew what Mercer would do, and he intended to use that knowledge to torment him.

"Unhand me," Mercer griped as two bobbies dragged him to his feet and secured his arms behind his back.

A moment later, Inspector Brickle's car came to a stop a few meters from the traffic jam. Brickle joined Bastian and the tactical team. After a brief exchange, Mercer and Bastian were loaded into the rear of an SUV. Brickle took a seat in the front.

"Who would have ever thought I'd be your alibi?" Brickle asked, eyeing Mercer. "If you hadn't been at the police station before the call came in, I might be inclined to believe you were part of this. But I know you aren't. And in light of recent developments, I may even be inclined to believe someone has a vendetta against you."

"No shit," Mercer snapped.

Brickle looked at Bastian. "Mr. Clarke, we haven't met, but you have questionable taste in friends. Explain to me why I shouldn't have you both tossed into the clink until this matter is sorted."

"This is the second explosion this week. Julian's the target. Once your team reviews the footage, I'm sure you'll be able to verify Jules' story."

"It's being done as we speak." Brickle blew out a breath. "You should have said something instead of rushing off. We might have been able to stop this. A few agents and several officers were injured."

Mercer shook his head. "You wouldn't have believed me."

"Perhaps not."

Mercer struggled to turn in the seat. "Unhook me."

Surprisingly, Brickle acquiesced.

"I still want the agent's name," Mercer said.

"I'm not authorized to share that with you. Just know, the matter is being investigated. You're a civilian. You don't have the authority to run through the streets, shooting at people. This is England. Remember, we call for civility here."

"Is this what you call civility? You phoned with news. I still haven't heard what it is."

"The status of your wife's case has changed. It is now considered a top priority, along with those other cases you asked about."

Mercer and Bastian exchanged glances. This was progress, but Mercer loathed the idea of the police mucking things up again. This would make his own investigation that much more difficult to conduct.

A moment later, Brickle took a call. "You're free to go, but don't get too confident. If you cross the line, we will arrest you."

"Go ahead and try. I dare you."

THIRTEEN

"You were his target," Bastian said.

"Or his patsy."

"When do you think he placed the device? It could have happened at any point after the exchange, but I'm guessing he did it right before the police received the tip. He was watching us that afternoon. I suppose we know why."

"How did he know we'd be there?" Mercer asked. Tired of feeling exposed, the pair ducked into a café.

"You said he's been tracking you," Bastian offered.

"I would have seen him or felt his presence. I didn't notice him until Yancy left. The bastard didn't follow me."

"Are you certain?"

"The bomber followed Yancy. Yancy could be working with him. It would explain a lot."

"Then why didn't the detective chief inspector have you jailed? Wouldn't that make things easier?"

Mercer snorted. "Where's the challenge in that?"

Deciding not to open that can of worms, Bastian

pushed ahead with the facts they possessed. "The device used today couldn't have been much larger than a pipe bomb. The blast was contained. The police had ample time to evacuate civilians. That's a good sign. As far as we know, there weren't any civilian casualties."

"We know the bomber is connected to Michelle's killer, and he takes joy in hurting innocents. Those measures were designed to toy with us, not spare lives."

"How could the bomber be certain you'd even hear about the threat and arrive on the scene? Frankly, Jules, you are not that predictable."

"He must have known I was at the police station. The call didn't come in until after I arrived, and the bomb didn't detonate until I entered the park to check out the scene." Mercer's eyes narrowed. "He was inside the park. He saw me. He wanted to make certain I saw him too."

"He didn't fire on you, did he?"

"No."

Bastian powered on the tablet he carried and glanced around the café. Once he was positive no one was paying him any attention, he opened the remote feed to view the camera footage from outside the park. "Nothing but fuzz. These are the only captured images." He held the tablet out to Mercer. "You look like you're trying to escape the scene of a crime."

"I wasn't. The bobbies know that."

"They do, but I think that flies in the face of the bomber's plan. He wanted you to be blamed."

"I winged him. There could be a blood trail. The authorities could swab it for DNA. He should be in the system, assuming he served." Without waiting, Mercer marched out of the café and back to the last place he remembered seeing the bomber.

The bomb unit was assessing the damage. Sweeps were being conducted for secondary devices. Uniformed officers were canvassing the area and questioning witnesses.

Mercer crossed the street and headed away from the park. When he located a patch of dark red, he knelt down. It was still wet. He scanned the ground in front of him, hoping to find another blood drop.

"Check for a trail," Mercer ordered when Bastian came up behind him.

"Do I look like a bloodhound?" Bas quipped. After a few meters, another spot of red marred the concrete. "Found one." He continued down the path for several blocks until the trail went cold at the curb. "He must have hitched a ride."

"Or he had an accomplice waiting." Mercer righted himself and wiped his palms on his trousers. "See what you can pull up."

"Don't you think we should inform the authorities?"

"Why? They didn't inform us of a psycho in our midst." Mercer's eye twitched, and he sucked in a breath while he slowly counted to ten.

"We'll need their assistance running the DNA. I might be able to work a few miracles with a computer, but I'm no scientist." Bastian glanced back at the flashing lights and official government vehicles. He knew the police wouldn't bother looking for evidence until the bomb experts cleared the area. Unfortunately, Great Britain had seen its fair share of bombings, so the authorities had protocols in place to deal with the risks. "Do you think the patrol officers realized you wounded the bomber?"

Mercer turned around, clocking the search pattern. "I should have mentioned it when they had me in cuffs. I wasn't thinking. That was an oversight. They need to know with whom we are dealing, if they don't already."

"Jules, we can call in a tip. Right now, we should get out of here."

"Not yet. They need to know who's responsible." Mercer strode toward the police. He gave the officers a basic description of the bomber, the direction in which he traveled, and the approximate time he left the park. "He was hurt. The bullet glanced across his back, but it did some damage." Mercer pointed at the blood drop. "The trail ends a few blocks ahead. Inspector Brickle has more details."

"How do you know this, sir?"

"Ask him."

"Okay." The officer looked uncertain. "I need you to remain for further questioning." He pointed at a parked police car. "Step over there. The detective chief inspector will have more questions for you."

"Will do, sir." Bastian led Mercer to the spot the officer indicated. As soon as the police turned their backs, Bastian jerked his chin to the side.

"I thought you were in favor of working with the authorities," Mercer muttered.

"I am. That's why I just saved them from dealing with you."

Before Mercer could say anything to the contrary, Bastian's phone rang. The analyst frowned and answered. He waited half a second and handed it to the commander. "It's for you."

Bastian kept his eyes on the police officers as they continued on their previous path to ward off civilians and establish a more secure perimeter. When no other police officers appeared, the pair took a sharp right and continued to walk away. Assuming the bus was running on schedule, it'd be the cleanest and most efficient means of disappearing. They could get off at any stop, split up, and disappear.

"That was a close call," the voice said in Mercer's ear. "If you'd taken the shot half a second sooner, we might not be having this conversation."

"Who is this?"

"Kills are supposed to be conducted in stealth. A silenced gun at close range. A knife to an artery. A needle in the neck. Have you forgotten everything we were taught?"

Mercer latched on to one word. *We.* "A bomb in a park? Isn't that too theatrical?"

"Desperate times, Julian. I needed to get your attention. You can't escape me. If you try again, there will be a rising death toll. Keep this phone on you, or I might have to turn my focus to Bastian or Hans. You must realize by now that I can get to them. I can get to anyone. I proved that by slaughtering your wife. And you don't want another death on your hands. This is between us. Keep it that way."

"Show yourself," Mercer bellowed, drawing unwanted attention from passersby.

"Not yet. Thanks to you, I'm at a disadvantage. Once we're on an even playing field, I'll make myself known. It's best you take this time to prepare for war, commander. I'm coming for you."

The caller hung up, and Mercer scanned the area. "We need an ID. He's escalating, and he wants me." Requesting police assistance might set the bomber off, but without their help, Mercer might not be able to identify the sicko fast enough. "He killed Michelle." The words barely registered. He felt the meaning more than he comprehended it. "I will end him."

"What did he want, Jules?"

"To issue a warning. We're going to war."

FOURTEEN

Tonight, Mercer was antsy. He kept his head on a swivel. Even remaining in the paranoid seat, as Lucie dubbed it, wasn't enough to provide peace of mind. The man responsible for the explosion this afternoon admitted to killing Michelle, and he was in the wind. The bastard was keeping tabs on his team. Mercer couldn't let that stand. He had to act.

He fought to remain still. Fidgeting would tip off any casual observer that he was nervous, and he didn't do nervous, at least not to any discernible extent as far as the outside world was concerned. He needed to move. To fight. To kill. His entire focus was on finding this bastard and bleeding him dry. Waiting inside the pub for DCI Yancy might be a waste of time, but Mercer needed answers. However, if he discovered Yancy was working with the killer, the copper would have no hope of surviving the encounter.

"Are you okay?" Lucie asked, reaching for a glass and the bottle of Irish whiskey.

"Yeah." His gaze settled on her for a moment before

returning to the blurred view through the frosted window. "Just some soda water, pet."

She cocked an eyebrow. "That's a new one." She put down the liquor bottle and reached for the spray to fill a glass with sparkling water. "Care for a twist?"

"You decide."

She let out an uneasy laugh. "I'd say you're anxious to talk to Argus. I have some of the pink stuff in the back if your stomach's in knots." She brushed her fingers against the back of his hand, and he jerked at the unexpected contact. "Easy, soldier." She smiled and leaned in closer. "For someone who's fine, you're rather jumpy. It's still early. If Argus drops by tonight, it won't be for another couple of hours. You can relax. He doesn't bite."

Mercer lifted the glass and took a sip. "Thanks."

For the next few hours, Lucie kept her distance, much to Mercer's relief. He didn't want the psychopath to target anyone else, which is why he distanced himself from his team. But unlike the K&R specialists, Lucie would be defenseless should the killer set his sights on her. He didn't want any other casualties weighing on his conscience. Absently, he rubbed his thumb against his bare ring finger. He always carried his wedding ring, but he only wore it when visiting the cemetery. Perhaps he would start wearing it regularly. It wasn't like his love could be exploited as a weakness.

Mercer allowed his mind to pursue these random musings while he stared out the window. When he spotted Yancy coming down the street, he scooted forward an inch so his back no longer rested against the wall. He wanted to be ready should the detective decide to bolt, but Yancy entered the tavern and selected a stool near the other end of the bar.

Slowly, Mercer stood. His focus remained out the

window, but he didn't spot a tail. While Yancy drummed his palms against the counter, waiting for Lucie or the bartender to fill his glass, Mercer went out the front door. He scanned both sides of the street for signs of the bomber. The area was clear, so he went back inside and took a seat beside Yancy.

"You must have brass ones," Yancy said, not bothering to turn. "I take it this isn't a coincidence."

"Call it what you will."

"I gave you the documents. Now what do you want? I heard you were at the scene of the explosion."

"We need to talk."

"So talk."

Mercer hesitated. He didn't like the exposure. Sure, he spent several long nights at the pub, but that was even more reason to be cautious. "I still don't trust you or the bloody lot you employ."

"That's your problem." Yancy nodded at the bartender who poured bourbon into a glass and placed it on the counter. When the bartender was no longer within earshot, Yancy swiveled to face Mercer. "I heard you paid Inspector Brickle a visit."

"Yes."

"Well, out with it then."

"Tell me about your task force. Why is MI5 involved? How many murders have occurred?" Mercer's eyes darted back and forth, assessing the area for threats or interlopers.

"Since you're asking those questions, you already know what's at stake. You weren't the first to lose a loved one. You were just another name in a long list. Too long, if you ask me. But we had to be careful. Each one of these homicides occurred under, shall we say, special circumstances. The cases aren't linked. There is no discernible connection, but they've been happening steadily for the last few years. MI5 brought it to my attention that these murders could be connected, but nothing indicates it. Our agencies were ordered to work together to investigate."

"And?"

"And there's no proof." Yancy downed his drink and signaled for another one. "How'd you know I'd come here?"

"You paid with a credit card."

"Is there anything you can't access?"

"Plenty." Mercer's thoughts were going in too many directions to count. "Brickle said an agent signed out the files concerning Michelle's murder investigation, but he wouldn't give me a name."

"I don't know it off the top of my head. Why does it matter?"

"Because if I'm to believe you aren't responsible for tampering with the evidence, someone else on your task force is. I need to know who. Give me a name."

Yancy smiled, his eyes settling on Lucie who was coming out of the storeroom with a few jars of olives. She put them on a shelf behind the bar.

"You found him," she said, eyeing Mercer. "Told you Argus would show up in a day or two. Would you gentlemen care for some privacy? You can go upstairs."

"I don't think—" Yancy began, but Mercer interrupted.

"That would be lovely."

She looked around, grabbed the bottle of hooch from the back shelf, along with two glasses, and handed them to Yancy. Then she lifted the wooden flap. "You know your way around up there." She gave the detective a look. "Be hospitable. Julian needs your help."

"You shouldn't talk to strangers," Yancy said. "We'll talk about this later, darling." Then he led the way through the curtain to the rear staircase.

"Are you sure you're all right?" Lucie asked Mercer. He nodded, and she clapped him on the shoulder. "You need anything, I'll be right here."

"If there's trouble, let us know."

She grinned. "Are you expecting trouble?"

"Always."

"Then you better behave. And don't break anything, or I'll kick your arse."

FIFTEEN

"Stay away from Lucie," Yancy warned as soon as he and Mercer went up the stairs. "She's been dealt a shitty hand. You don't need to make it worse. I can only assume your presence in this pub is your way of emphasizing the threat you made inside my home, but I won't tolerate it. I will lock you up or take whatever measures are necessary to keep her safe."

Mercer smirked. This new development was interesting. It might be the leverage he needed to ensure Yancy remained compliant, knowing the detective's weakness would make identifying the killer and his cohorts easier. And, at the moment, discovering the man's identity was the only thing on Mercer's mind.

The two men settled into the front room of Lucie's apartment. It was a tiny, cluttered place. "I don't care what can be proven or what the system deems proper," Mercer said. "I want to know the truth. The bomber is the same man who killed my wife."

"How do you know that?"

"He told me. Who is he?"

"I assure you, I don't know."

"You must know something."

"Someone strategically placed in the government is doing what they can to conceal certain facts related to the string of homicides. Even the chaps at MI5 don't know the whole truth. Your people obtained the information via your previous connection with military intelligence. What did they disclose to you?"

Mercer frowned, not liking the shift in the questioning. "They provided the same intel as the Met, which I was granted only because someone twisted your arm. Tell me what was removed from your bloody notebook."

Yancy filled both glasses and slid one across the table. "Farnsworth spoke to someone the same afternoon your wife was killed. It might have been a neighbor, but whoever he spoke to said someone else entered your home."

"Who?"

"I don't know. It's been ages."

"It hasn't been that long." It felt like yesterday. The wounds were still fresh.

"I don't recall details, but I do recall a discrepancy in what we assumed was an airtight case. If I'm thinking clearly, the only fact that didn't fit with our theory was the man's hair color. He was a dirty blond. Tall and fit, like you. He might have even been wearing the same clothing you were on that dark day. We marked him as an unreliable eyewitness and planned to question him again."

"Why didn't you tell me this sooner? You lied. You said you didn't know what was missing."

"I don't know what's missing," Yancy argued. "After you banged down my door, I thought it'd be pertinent to look into these matters before you came back and did something else unsettling."

"Don't tempt me."

"I found a notation in the official report saying a witness was unavailable for further comment. I'm guessing the witness's information is what was removed from the notebooks since his name and contact information isn't recorded anyplace else. But that's just a guess."

"Likely story." Mercer sat up straighter, his muscles growing rigid. "Who is this witness?"

"We don't know. Farnsworth should have conducted the follow-up, but that never happened. Brickle tried canvassing the neighborhood, but he never located the witness in question. The man disappeared, and since Farnsworth didn't write his name in any official report, there was nothing else we could do."

"Do you think Farnsworth spoke to the killer?" Mercer asked, finding it difficult to follow the DCI's train of thought. Yancy reached for the bottle, and Mercer snatched it out of his grasp. "I want you clear, detective."

Yancy picked up the other glass and downed the contents, giving Mercer a smug, self-satisfied look. "I don't think Farnsworth spoke to the killer directly. But I believe the killer thought Farnsworth was getting too close. He was the only officer able to identify the witness. Should we encounter the witness again, we might have managed to extricate even more useful information out of him. So the killer tracked down Farnsworth and made it look like an accident."

"What's your basis for thinking that?"

"This is speculation. Plain and simple. But no one else was injured in the alleged fight Farnsworth was called to break up, and that never sat right with me. Maybe I'm jaded or senile. I imagine someone like you and the lot you run with would know how to put a man down permanently with a blow like that."

"So now I killed Farnsworth?" Mercer scoffed.

"Let's cut the bullshit. I've spent the last several hours doing nothing but reviewing footage from the park. It's no coincidence the location of our clandestine meeting was also the precise location some nutter decided to detonate a device. I scrolled back through the feed. You chased him out of the park after I made the drop-off. When were you planning on telling me he was there that day?"

"I wasn't."

"Whoever this wanker is, he's a soldier who must have lost the plot, probably after rolling around too long in the sandbox. He knows you. Whatever is going on right now is about you. It isn't about your wife or anyone else this fucker killed. This is about you. And as far as I can tell, he's turning my city into his battleground. What does he want?"

"I don't know."

"Do you know who he is?"

"Not yet. I'm working on it. Your mates recovered his DNA this afternoon. And I'm still not certain you aren't assisting him in some manner."

"How dare you," Yancy snapped. "I want him gone as quickly as possible."

"Then help me. I need everything you have on the killings."

"I already gave you everything I possibly can. You need to work faster. Lives are at stake."

"Don't you think I fucking know that?"

Yancy grabbed the liquor bottle from Mercer's hand. "Based on agency interference and the things I've seen, this wanker must have come from military operations. He's trained and deadly. He's proven it many times over." Yancy took a swig from the bottle.

"I'd wager so are you. My hands are tied. The Met can't do much. We don't have enough evidence. This investigation has been ongoing for years, and we can't even prove it's one man."

"It might be a team." Mercer recalled previous conversations with Bastian and Parker.

Yancy swallowed another gulp. "You mean there might be more than one? How can you possibly think that?"

"The camera interference. The killer utilized a jammer or some other distortion device, but we can't discount the possibility someone might be assisting off-site. Someone followed you the day of the drop-off. The killer knows things that require extensive reconnaissance, and that's a difficult feat for one man to achieve."

"But it is possible?"

"Yes."

"The camera distortion, is that how you'd do it?"

Mercer nodded.

"All right," Yancy took a final sip from the bottle and put it down, "what do you need?"

Mercer was taken aback by the detective's willingness to help. Only seconds ago, he said he had done all he could. During their previous encounter, Yancy was far from accommodating. Granted, the detective agreed to the drop, but that was only due to the potential risk Mercer posed to Yancy's loved ones. So why was the detective suddenly so willing to help?

"The files. Everything. And the name of the MI5 agent who requested the file transfer," Mercer replied.

"You have everything. I left the last bits in that envelope beneath the park bench."

"Except the name."

"I'll get it."

"I need whatever you can get from the other half of

your task force. If what you say is true about someone in the government covering up these crimes, I can't trust the intel MI5 has provided my team."

"I can try, but they haven't been cooperative in the past. You might have better luck. They responded to your initial request."

"Is that why Brickle and the rest of the inspectors are convinced I murdered my wife?"

"You have to see it from our perspective."

"No, I don't."

"You fit the profile. You had the means, the opportunity, and, if we're being honest, marriage is hard. It could lend itself to motive."

"I would never." Mercer's insides clenched. He remembered her smile and the smell of her hair. He could never hurt her.

"Maybe not intentionally, but you must have seen things and done things. Atrocities like that can haunt a man. I'd know. This job cost me my marriage. It's not unreasonable to assume a situation could have escalated. A simple spat could have caused you to lose control."

Despite the detective's offer to assist, Mercer couldn't help but feel the copper was still trying to determine if Mercer was responsible. The words went through his mind, but he clamped his mouth shut. They would not leak out. Not here. Not in the presence of a potential enemy. But he felt them in every fiber of his being. He was the reason Michelle was dead.

"You look like you've seen a ghost," Yancy said. "Did I bring up bad memories?"

"Has the killer made any threats?"

"Besides tipping us off about the bombs? No. That's been about it. And before you ask, the calls have been anonymous. They are entirely untraceable."

"He's using a satellite phone. What about the blood trail he left at the latest scene? How long until the DNA results come back?"

"I heard tales of some man opening fire, but surveillance was on the fritz. Until now, I didn't realize it was you." Yancy snorted. "Shouldn't you be a better shot? I thought the SAS was a bunch of sharpshooting spies."

"Conditions weren't favorable." Mercer's eyes went even harder. "Since he's a soldier, his DNA has to be on file. You can run a comparison."

"This isn't some program on the telly. Tests take time, even when we prioritize. We should know something in the next few days."

"Assuming the bomber doesn't interfere." Several disconcerting thoughts played through Mercer's mind. "When we last spoke, you said you were afraid the police department has a leak."

"Aye."

"You should know I was at the station when the threat came in. The killer obtained my private number, which was given only to Inspector Brickle. You can't trust your people."

"Do you trust me?"

"Not in the least."

"That's only fair, seeing as how I feel the same about you."

"Fair warning, the killer might be stalking you."

Yancy paled. "I haven't noticed anyone lurking, except you."

"You responded to another bomb threat a little over a week ago. That was the same evening I first went to your home. I no longer believe that was a coincidence."

"You were waiting for me?"

"I told you I visited your cottage a time before."

"Right." Yancy blinked, considering some things. "But that probably has little to do with me. It sounds like he might be trying to pin the bombings on you. You're in his way."

"He put me there." Mercer was getting twitchy. Too many oddities occurred concerning the bomber and Yancy. "You need to pay attention. He might have plans for you."

"Sorry, but they don't train us to deal in tradecraft or military maneuvers. I hate to admit it, but you might be the only one capable of putting an end to these killings. He's targeting the families of servicemen. He's repeating a pattern. I assume he killed his own family and is now doing the same to others, but that's speculation. It's also possible he has a vendetta against the specific men he targeted. Payback for some perceived injustice, perhaps? Do you know anyone who might have an agenda?"

"My team is compiling a list, even though that should have been your job from the beginning."

"Like I said, it's speculation. We have no proof."

"You have more than a dozen victims. That's your proof. More than enough. You should have stopped this before the bastard targeted Michelle." The anger grew to an unbearable level, and Mercer ripped the bottle out of the detective's hand and threw it against the wall. He wouldn't tolerate this prick getting hammered. It was bad enough Yancy was ordering Mercer around and pointing out the ex-soldier's failures, but it was even more emasculating to hear these things from the lips of a drunken fool. "You have a responsibility to the citizens of London. You are supposed to protect them. You were supposed to protect her when I wasn't here. I should have never left. If I had known..." He poked Yancy in the chest. "If your incompetent feeble-minded lot informed the public of the danger, I would have stopped him before he took her. So as far as I'm concerned, this is your fucking fault."

"Julian," Lucie's sharp tone snapped Mercer out of his rage-fueled diatribe before his words turned into actions, "that's enough." She stepped into the flat and pointed at the door. "Get out."

His eyes blazed, but he stepped reluctantly away from Yancy. This wasn't the time or place. He would speak to the detective elsewhere.

"It's okay, darling," Yancy said. "He's right. Our inaction protected a killer. It's another Whitechapel, all over again."

"There's another ripper?" Lucie asked.

"No, just a trained killer on the hunt," Mercer spat.

"And he killed your wife?" she asked.

Mercer nodded.

"You have to do something, Dad," Lucie said.

Mercer blinked at the word. Argus Yancy was quite the enigma. No wonder the detective was desperate to shield Lucie from danger.

"Actually, Mr. Mercer is going to help us," Yancy said. "Isn't that right?"

"Indeed." He gave Yancy another searing look. "You better be on the level."

SIXTEEN

Mercer blew into his closed fist and stared at the screen. Despite his objections, he, Bastian, and Donovan were settled around a table at one of the dodgier inns. The DNA results came back blank, as if the killer never existed or wasn't part of any database.

"We know he was an operative," Bastian said. "His name and personal details are unknown. There's no photo ID because that would make things too bloody simple. I reached out to our contacts and alerted them of the wolf in their midst, but no one is acknowledging this, even though blood was found at the site of the bombing yesterday which I bet matches one of Her Majesty's highly trained operatives."

"He's a bloody terrorist," Donovan hissed. "Nothing more than a mad dog. He needs to be put down."

"I imagine they are hoping to do so quietly, in-house," Bastian said. "If they bothered listening to a word I said."

"He could be British Army intelligence," Mercer speculated.

"More likely, Special Air Service," Donovan replied. "We had more interaction with our own kind than anyone else."

Bastian reached for his lighter, flicking it open and closed several times. He had a cigarette tucked behind his ear, but he quit, which Mercer reminded him only moments earlier. "He might still be active. Parker thinks the lengthier pauses between murders could be due to deployment. Some missions take months. We know this. We lived this."

Donovan rubbed the bridge of his nose and circled the room. Every few minutes, he would glance out the blinds for signs of a tail. He was used to viewing things from the other side of a sniper scope, so he reasoned the killer might have Mercer and the rest of the team in his sights. "Do you think his CO realizes they have a psychopath in their midst?"

"He might suspect, but the mission comes first. The killer does his job well. I doubt he'd ever question an order, and he wouldn't leave witnesses around. He'd eliminate all targets and any potential hostiles in the area. He'd make a clean sweep of it," Mercer surmised. "Those skills are beneficial under most circumstances."

"Someone is willing to turn a blind eye to this. They'll keep it up until it becomes obvious he's killing for sport. The fact that he's limiting his targets probably helps." Bas reached for a printout. "Parker and I have spoken at length. We're guessing he was assigned to a support unit which assisted our team. He probably had similar run-ins with everyone else he targeted. That's how he crossed paths with us." Bastian looked at Mercer. "We're just not certain why he fixated on you. Parker believes it has to do with our work now. Unlike the other survivors, you're still very much in the game, even if it isn't in service of the crown."

Mercer blinked. "Neither of you should be here. He made his demands clear. This is between him and me."

"Let him come," Donovan said. "We'll be ready."

"Jules, we function best as a team," Bastian added.

"This isn't an op. I don't need a team. I just need to know who the bloody fuck he is. Then I'm going to trap him and kill him. You said there was crossover between him and the other troops. We have a basic physical description and this rubbish. It shouldn't be hard to pinpoint a name." Mercer sifted through the files. "Where's the list of possible suspects?"

"It's not a small number. We've worked with dozens of units. There is a lot of overlap on missions. We crisscrossed so much, the killer could be anyone." Donovan looked to Bastian for help.

"I've made some inquiries to determine who was stateside at the time of the killings. Since we are no longer part of the SAS, accessing highly classified intel which could impact current ops is not an easy ask. So instead, I've started checking with members of the other teams to see who is presently on holiday and was at the time of the murders."

"The killer will hear about it," Mercer warned. "He might be one of the people you contacted."

"Might be." Bastian removed his cigarette from behind his ear and tapped the tip on the tabletop.

"You shouldn't be poking about. He already threatened you. We need to treat this like a ransom. He needs to believe I will agree to his terms. If he realizes we're looking for him, he'll want to end this before we end him."

"With all due respect," Donovan said, "you're wrong. Every victim was related to a highly decorated soldier. He's pitting himself against his peers. Perhaps he has a chip on his shoulder. Or maybe he wants someone to stop him, and only the best will do. Right now, he thinks that's you."

"He wants to face off against you, Jules," Bastian said. "You're his white whale."

Mercer stared a hole through the wall. "He killed my wife because he believes I'm his equal. What do you think he'll do to the rest of you if he thinks you're interfering with his plans?"

"I'm willing to take the chance," Bastian said.

"What about Hans? He's in no condition to fight this war, and this plonker knows it. He'll use it to his advantage. We can't risk it."

"Let us worry about Hans. You need to look through these profiles and see if anyone hits a nerve. Michelle knew him, Jules. That means you do too."

"Are we certain?"

"Everything points to it."

Mercer reached for the list of suspects. "I tried to keep her away from this life."

"I know." Bastian put the unlit cigarette back in the box and reached for a bag of crisps. He needed to do something, and smoking would result in a swift arse kicking. "But Michelle had a kind heart. She welcomed us into your home as your brothers on the rare occasions your work life and home life overlapped. Remember Getty's funeral?"

Michelle went with him, even though he told her there was no need. But she always wanted to support him, despite the circumstances. Any one of those events could have put her on the killer's radar and into his crosshairs, as if Mercer's stellar record hadn't been tantalizing enough to draw this bastard into her world.

Opening his wallet, he dug through the tiny compartment for a safety deposit box key. He still owned the house where she'd been killed, but he hadn't stepped foot inside since her murder. Bastian, Donovan, and Hans had gone several times to collect his belongings and look for clues. After Mercer's dismissal from the SAS, Bastian made a final trip to the home, closing it up for the foreseeable future. The keys to the house and important documents were in a lockbox at the bank.

"I'm going home. If she knew him, we should start at the beginning. I'll look through our wedding video and guestbook. She kept them in the study. We'll go from there."

"All right." Bastian clapped him on the shoulder. "Care for some company?"

"I need to do this alone." Mercer glanced at Donovan. "Stay close to Hans. This bastard is nothing but a coward who picks on the weak."

"Copy that."

"You're worried about DCI Yancy, aren't you?" Bastian asked, reading Mercer's mind.

"I don't believe the killer followed me to the park. I believe he followed Yancy. He must have known of Yancy's connection to the tavern. That's how he picked up my trail outside and why he planted the bomb. He never intended for it to kill me, but if it did, it would have demonstrated I wasn't a worthy adversary." Mercer went to the door. "He should have thought twice about delaying the detonation because I'll be the last bloody adversary this bastard ever has."

Slamming the door, Mercer scanned the vicinity. The coast appeared clear, but Donovan made a fair point. The killer could be set up hundreds of meters away, watching through the scope of a rifle. After searching the windows of nearby buildings for lens glare, Mercer got into his car and drove away.

Unsettling thoughts weaved their way through his

mind. He invited this arsehole into his home. He introduced his wife to her killer. The thought sickened him. He swallowed the bile which rose in his throat. That man would die, slowly and painfully. There was no question about it. He just didn't know how to go on living with the knowledge he welcomed this evil into Michelle's life and his mistake cost her everything.

He tried to shake the morose thoughts away. He couldn't worry about them now. He had to put an end to the murders and bombings, but more than anything, he had to keep his promise. He had to kill her killer.

After picking up his house keys, he slipped on his wedding band. The coolness of the metal against his skin was oddly reassuring. Pleasant memories flooded him as he parked in front of the house. For a moment, he sat in the car and stared at the front door. He remembered the giddiness of returning home after a mission, the way she would launch herself into his arms as soon as he stepped foot inside, the taste of her lips, the scent of her skin, and the way she wrapped herself around him. Even though he knew it was different now, that everything was different, when he unlocked the front door and stepped inside, the tiniest part of him hoped this nightmare was a lie and she'd greet him like she always did.

Instead, he was met by nothing but darkness. He fumbled to hit the light switch, taken aback by the stale, dusty smell. The furniture was covered in thick white sheets, as if the house were full of ghosts. And in a way, it was. Thankfully, Bastian had the foresight to keep the power and water turned on or else the place really would be overrun by apparitions.

Mercer took an unsteady breath, dropping the box of potential suspects on the floor. His heart raced. Cursing, he stormed through the living room and into the study, stopping abruptly in the doorway. This was her space. She'd sit in here for hours and read while he worked on mission logs or reviewed briefing notes. A teacup sat on the end table. He couldn't help but look around, as if she just abandoned it. The contents had long since evaporated, leaving a permanent stain in the bottom of the cup. A smudge of the rosy pink gloss she'd worn that afternoon rimmed the edge in a perfect half-moon.

He blinked several times on the verge of a breakdown. *Not now, soldier*, he thought. Reminding himself of his mission, he went to the shelves and found their wedding video and guestbook. With the items in hand, he returned to the living room and ripped the sheets off the furniture. Angrily balling them up, he tossed them into a corner. He stabbed at the power button on the television, pushed play on the video, and settled onto the sofa.

As the tape played, he focused on nothing but the appearance of guests, checking off the names in the book as the footage played. Mercer kept a tally. By the end, he was certain everyone, aside from the staff, signed the book. Removing the burner phone from his pocket, he took photos of each page and sent the list to Bastian. Since the authorities insisted Michelle knew her killer, it wouldn't hurt to make sure every potential suspect was on the list.

A moment later, his phone buzzed. "I'll sort through this. From just a glance, I already see some overlap," Bastian said, his voice cool and professional, the same way it sounded during ransom negotiations.

"Brilliant. Let me know when it's complete."

"Will do."

Mercer rewound the wedding video and closed the guestbook, turning to make sure the curtains were drawn. He didn't want or need an audience. He craved solitude, and his team would make sure he had it for as long as he wanted, unless the killer surfaced.

He rubbed his temples and hit play, staring at the screen. He couldn't stop himself. There she was in a beautiful white gown, light pink flowers in her hair, and a wicked smile that made his breath catch. She blew a kiss at him, and his chest constricted to the point of pain. The screen went dark for the seventh time, and he resisted the urge to replay the footage again. Instead, he flipped through the book on his lap.

The ceremony was small. They had sixty guests. Once the relatives were removed from the equation, the suspect list dwindled further. Mercer convinced himself he had to watch the video again to make sure no one crashed the party, but if he were being honest, he just wanted to see her and hear her voice, even though it shredded his heart and threatened his sanity.

Bastian was running profiles on the guests. If the killer was at Mercer's wedding, Bastian would find him. The analyst also took the initiative and checked the records for official military ceremonies the Mercers attended. Michelle could have crossed paths with the killer at any one of those functions. The more Mercer thought about it, the more distraught he became. Was the killer someone he once considered a friend? Was it someone he trusted on the battlefield? Was he someone Mercer trusted around his wife? Or was this nothing but conjecture dreamt up by a bunch of sadistic detectives who wanted to do nothing but torment him further?

The possibilities seemed endless. The endeavor hopeless. Hopelessness was all he had known for the last couple of years. He couldn't let himself have hope, at least not yet. He was too stubborn for that. And he would never accept defeat. It wasn't a word in his vocabulary. He would dole out retribution despite the cost. The road through hell was long and winding. Either he or the killer wouldn't make it out alive.

He hit play again and again, remembering everything about that day. It ripped his chest open, the wounds fresh and bleeding. When he could no longer see on account of the tears, he turned off the telly and went up the stairs to the guest bathroom. He couldn't go into their bedroom, and he wouldn't dare go near the kitchen. But he wasn't ready to leave.

After turning on the tap, he let the sink fill with cold water. He scrubbed his face, fighting back the emotions. Now wasn't the time. One day soon that would change.

By the time he emerged from the bathroom, he was exhausted. The coldness of his skin matching the internal cold he felt. He went into the guestroom, finding more ghostly figures. He pulled the sheets from the furniture, the dresser covered in little knickknacks. Rarely, did they use this room, but it still contained her presence. He climbed onto the bed and closed his eyes. Now that he was home, he didn't want to leave. He didn't want to leave her again.

SEVENTEEN

Mercer rubbed his eyes and leaned back in the chair. He'd spent hours building a profile. The killer was slightly taller than Julian, with dark blond or light brown hair, and he smoked clove cigarettes, kreteks as they were more commonly known. They were Indonesian in origin. Mercer figured the killer must have spent some time in the country to have picked up a taste for them.

Every SpecOps member had to go through rigorous training, but since the killer used IEDs to draw attention to himself, Mercer wondered if bomb disposal or demolition was the killer's specialty. Making a note, he flipped through the list he made.

Page after page contained names of other SAS members. From what Bastian provided, Mercer hoped to narrow it down further. Michelle knew the killer. That meant they met at least once before. Even though identities of SAS team members remained secret, it wasn't uncommon to socialize. Perhaps he and Michelle had attended a barbeque or birthday party that he didn't recall. Potentially any one of the names on the list could be the killer.

Indonesia, Mercer thought. He already crossed off several men based on physical characteristics. Too bad he didn't have complete service records in front of him. He phoned Bastian and relayed this newest tidbit and provided the updated list.

"That helps a lot, Jules. It might not have been an op. The killer might have grown-up there."

"Perhaps." Disconnecting, Mercer was going through the list again when the phone rang. "Bugger." He reached for the phone.

"Home, sweet home," a voice said.

Mercer went to the window, but he didn't see anyone. "What do you want?" He reached for a RF reader and scanned his house. He didn't think it was bugged, but how did this arsehole know where he was?

"Nothing, yet." The killer hung up.

After completing a check for bugs, Mercer phoned Bastian. "He knows I'm here. I want to know how."

"What did he say? We can rendezvous at your location."

"Negative. It is imperative you stay away. Just get on those cameras."

*   *   *

Mercer stood outside his house and stared at the front door. His thumb rubbed against his wedding band. It was a habit. He never wore his ring in the field, but he always had it with him. He wouldn't step foot on the property without wearing it. It was a tether to normalcy. It meant he belonged here.

"Do you see me?" Mercer said into the phone.

"Move a step to your right," Alexis Parker insisted. Bastian hacked into the area's CCTVs and patched that access to Parker. "Okay, you're invisible. Keep going."

Mercer took a few steps forward. "What about now?"

"Still nothing. I'll let you know when I see you."

"Okay." Mercer continued on his path. Initially, he tried performing this exercise with Bastian to see if it was possible to stroll through the neighborhood, enter the house, and leave without being detected, but after a few failed attempts and Bas's annoying commentary concerning ways to manipulate camera feeds, Mercer decided he'd rather deal with the headstrong American. "I'm inside." He crossed to the coffee table and looked at the blown-up area map and marked the cameras blind spots. "Let's reset and go again."

"Sure. Let me know when you're ready. I need to grab a refill."

"Don't dawdle."

"It's barely five a.m. here, so screw off."

"It's sod off," he corrected.

She chuckled. "Screw off, sod off. Whatever."

"Birds." He went back outside to try again. It was early in the day, but the constant drizzle and chilling breeze encouraged those nearby to mind their business. After another two attempts, Mercer came to a conclusion. "The killer must have seen me return home. That's how he knew to call."

"Sounds like you have a stalker."

"No shit." But his mind was already onto something else. "When he came to kill my wife, he stayed in the blind spots. He didn't bypass or alter the surveillance feeds. He navigated around them."

"I'm sorry. If we'd known this sooner, I wouldn't have wasted so much time going through the footage."

"No matter."

"Were the vehicle registrations just as useless?"

"Yes." Mercer thought for a moment, remembering he agreed to meet DCI Yancy later. It had been four days since their tete-a-tete inside Lucie's flat. The London police might have made progress comparing the DNA to unsolved crimes. It wasn't much, but it might be enough to convince some higher-up to take action. "I'll be in contact again." Without bothering to say a proper goodbye, he hung up.

After updating Bastian on their latest findings, he rendezvoused with his team on the train. Mass transit was an easy way to scatter and disappear should a psychopath target them. It also limited points of entry, and since the three of them were armed and prepared for war, they weren't afraid of a confrontation. But the killer didn't materialize on the train. As far as Mercer could tell, the killer went to ground after the shooting outside the park. The bastard was probably holed up somewhere, licking his wounds and plotting revenge.

"I'll be staying at home," Mercer said. "Parker and I spent the last few hours reviewing blind spots throughout the neighborhood."

"It's residential, mate," Donovan said. "High-end surveillance isn't common like it is near the palace or the commercial districts."

Bastian glanced at Mercer. "You made notes?"

"Yes."

Bastian nodded. "I'll put our own cameras up on connecting streets and around your house. Are you sure about staying there? You'll be exposed."

"I can't leave until this is done. Plus, it'd be fitting if it ended where it began."

"Okay, we'll take care of it. Donovan will check for sniper's nests and the best perches. We'll run a threat assessment and figure out where to set up. If this bastard thinks the way we do, we must think the way he does. We'll get right on that evaluation. In the meantime, where are you meeting Yancy?" Bastian asked.

"Lucie's."

Donovan snorted. "Sounds like a terrible idea, mate."

"It wasn't mine." Mercer looked at Bastian. "How come we didn't know the detective had more offspring?"

"For all intents and purposes, he doesn't. Lucie's thirty-two, making her the oldest. Her birth certificate has no father listed, and Yancy didn't meet his wife until two years later. He must have knocked up Lucie's mum at university, or maybe the lass was a one-night stand."

"It could be a lie," Donovan said. "Are you certain she wasn't calling him daddy?"

Mercer frowned. "She believes he's her father."

"We could ask her mum."

Bastian shook his head. "The poor woman died five years ago, which was around the time Yancy started going to the pub. No paternity test was ever performed, at least not that I found. But he probably realized she was his kid and wanted to help out after her mum was gone. His marriage fell apart two years after that, which probably isn't a coincidence."

"Since Argus is her father, he should know better than to use her pub as a meeting place when a psycho is on the loose." Inwardly, Mercer cursed himself for endangering another innocent life and swore he would be damned if he let anything happen to Lucie.

"He's a copper, Jules," Bastian said. "They take care of their own, just like we take care of our own."

The announcement came over the intercom that the train was about to stop at the next station, and Mercer let out a breath. "That's my precise intention.

Tell Hans to get well. I hate to admit it, but we could use his expertise."

Donovan smiled. "He'll think that's the dog's balls."

* * *

"You look like you could use a stiff one, mate." Lucie didn't bother waiting before pouring the bourbon into a glass. "Argus likes his bourbon, and since he isn't here yet, you might as well help yourself to it."

Mercer took a sip. "Notice anything out of the ordinary?"

"Same as always. Why? Is there something I should know?"

"I shouldn't be here."

She laughed. "I agree. You're a lousy tipper."

"I'm serious."

"So am I." She smiled, her eyes went to the door. "Speak of the devil." She poured another glass and left the bottle on the counter.

Yancy slid onto the stool and picked up the glass. "Cheers." He downed the contents and rubbed a heavy hand down his face. "Any progress?"

Mercer's eyes darted around the pub. As usual, he chose the far corner for its tactical advantage. Despite everything, he was still unsure if he trusted the bobby. "We can't identify him. We have some leads, an estimation of his military record, but nothing solid. I haven't seen him since he escaped the park."

"How can you have his record and not his name?"

"Ask Her Majesty. It's protected. Classified."

"Was your identity classified when you were an operative?"

"Yes."

"His DNA isn't linked to any open cases. The killer left no physical evidence at any murder scene. It doesn't look like he committed any other crimes, or if he did, he was bloody meticulous."

"What about the possibility someone in your office is working with him?"

"Nothing concrete." Yancy removed a photocopied document from his pocket and handed the folded page to Mercer. "That's a copy of the evidence log. You wanted the name of the MI5 agent who accessed your wife's case file. There it is."

Mercer glanced at the name. It was Bastian's contact who pulled the file. According to the sign-out sheet, that agent signed for the file every time. "This isn't helpful."

"I told you it wouldn't be. Inspector Brickle told you the same thing." Yancy refilled his glass and took another drink. "You're wasting my time. How do I know the killer isn't one of your friends? You said you work with a team. It stands to reason one of them could arrange for the bombing when they knew you'd be at the station. Maybe that's why you only winged the killer. You wouldn't want to hurt one of your own."

"You're bleeding insane. The only people I trust are my mates."

"What's the expression? Thick as thieves? Killers must have an even stronger bond."

Mercer struggled to contain his fury. How many times would he have to defend himself or his team? Why couldn't the authorities get it through their thick skulls that he was the victim? "The last time we spoke, you said I might be the only one capable of stopping the killer. What changed?"

"As if you don't know."

"I don't."

"Right."

Mercer grabbed Yancy by the collar and yanked

him off the stool. "What happened?"

"Come off it. I know you broke into my office at work. You had your team wipe my computer after you poked around. Everything's gone. You made it clear you didn't trust me to investigate, but I never realized the lengths you'd go. And then you sit here," Yancy jerked free and smoothed his tie, "and pretend you have no idea why I'm so blooming upset."

"Was it just your computer?"

"It was the whole bloody system. Luckily, the data was backed up to an external server."

"That wasn't me. My team isn't responsible. If we poked around, we didn't do any damage. We wouldn't. That was him. He knows you're on to him. You need to watch yourself. And you need to stay away from me. We shouldn't be here. You should want better for your daughter. These visits could encourage him to use her as fodder. Stay away from here."

"I'm only here to look after her. You need to stay away."

"I'll make contact when I know more. I gave Brickle a number to call. The killer also has it. I'm stuck with that phone, so use it if you need assistance."

Without another word, Mercer left the pub. Almost immediately, he sensed someone watching. For the briefest moment, he spotted a man waiting across the street in a long overcoat and hat, but as the bus drove past, the man vanished. The killer wanted to toy with Mercer, and he planned to do so by targeting DCI Argus Yancy.

EIGHTEEN

The wind blew fiercely. Mercer turned his collar up to keep out the rain. It wasn't easy being a shadow, but it was a skill he perfected long ago. Unfortunately, the killer seemed to have perfected it as well.

After his last meeting with Yancy, Mercer informed Bas about the computer breach at the Metropolitan Police Service. Bastian parsed through the data, looking for altered or deleted intel. Military intelligence was informed of the breach and were assessing their own servers, but they had nothing to report. And if they did, they weren't sharing that information with the K&R specialists.

It was lunchtime when Argus Yancy stepped out of headquarters. He opened an umbrella and made his way to an official vehicle. While Argus folded the umbrella and climbed behind the wheel, Mercer unlocked his rental and got inside. When the detective chief inspector pulled away, Mercer glanced at the tracker on his screen to make sure it was active. Then he watched and waited.

Three minutes later, a black sedan pulled out of a nearby garage. It turned in the same direction Yancy traveled, and Mercer pursued. He'd seen a similar vehicle the morning he left Lucie's Tavern and a few times when he visited Hans at the hospital. But black sedans were common, and every time he checked the license plates, the numbers were always different. Even now, the car had a different plate than the previous two, but those were easy to switch with a few free seconds and a screwdriver.

Mercer followed the car, keeping a safe distance. If the killer was behind the wheel, hopefully he wouldn't expect to be followed. When stalking a subject, one rarely considered the possibility of being stalked. Still, Mercer was cautious of surprise attacks and had to assume the killer would be as well.

The blip on the monitor stopped. Yancy had a lunch meeting with several government officials to address the recent data breach. Security would be tight, but if the killer wanted to demonstrate his superior skills and prowess, this would be the perfect place to mount an assault. Given the recent threats and detonation, the bomb squad was on-site, having completed a full sweep of the building. They were now checking all parties who entered for suspicious devices.

The black car continued past the building, turning onto a side street. Mercer slowed, thankful for a crosswalk. While he waited for foot traffic to pass, he watched the black sedan pull into another parking structure. There was another entrance on a parallel street. As soon as he was able, Mercer crossed and entered through the other opening. He parked in the first available space and waited.

A few more vehicles entered, but the black sedan didn't leave. Mercer might have been incorrect in assuming the car belonged to the killer, but that was the only follow car he spotted.

Getting out of the vehicle, Mercer surveyed the nearby automobiles before going level by level in search of the black sedan. He found the vehicle two levels down, near the other entrance, but the license plate didn't match. The driver was no longer in sight, so Mercer placed his palm on the bonnet, feeling the warmth of the engine. This had to be the same car.

He scanned the garage for surveillance cameras. The killer utilized blind spots to minimize his chances of being identified. A support pillar blocked a few other cars from view. The plate from the black sedan was now attached to a red sports car.

Mercer was right, and he was getting closer. Taking to the streets, he knew it would be harder to conceal himself from the killer. The man he was pursuing knew precisely who he was. Mercer couldn't say the same, but he was determined to find out.

"Bas, I suspect another bomb threat is imminent. We need to be prepared to monitor incoming phone calls."

"I don't have access to the emergency services lines. But our mates at MI5 do."

"Is that wise?"

"Probably not, but we don't have a choice. Have you located the threat?"

"I'm close. He's here. I just have to find him. He wants to make a spectacle, turn the police into a laughingstock, which isn't a difficult feat to achieve."

"Be that as it may, the killer believes the group assembled is comprised of high-value targets. Do you think he'll bother calling in a threat? It'd be smarter to blow up the entire lot."

"True, but he likes a challenge. An explosion isn't personal. And he wants this to be personal." Mercer scanned the nearby buildings. "There are several vantage points. He might wait until the evacuation is underway and pick off his targets one by one."

"Every murder has been in close range. He always has the tactical advantage because he attacks unarmed, untrained civilians, but if he made a miscalculation or underestimated someone, it would be a close-quarters battle to the death. If he attacks Yancy or someone else at the meeting, I believe it'll be from close range."

"Agreed. I'll keep my eyes on the ground."

"Should I ring Donovan?"

"Negative. If this bastard slips away, we don't know where he might strike next. Should another threat surface, we'll have a better chance of preventing a tragedy if we remain spread out."

"Okay, Jules. Best of British."

Where are you? Mercer thought as he circled the building. The luncheon was being held inside a conference room. Security was tighter than usual. The killer would see this as another challenge. "Narcissist." The man he was hunting had hubris, which is why Mercer wasn't positive he wouldn't use a sniper rifle to strike from a distance. A difficult shot would prove his superiority as easily as any other stealth kill on the street.

As Mercer contemplated the building's structural weaknesses, he considered the possibility a bomb threat might be more than a threat. The device in the park detonated, injuring several first responders. And since the police were already out in force, another detonation wasn't out of the question.

Deciding to check for less obvious threats, despite the bomb squad's initial sweep, Mercer searched for alternate points of entry. There were several, but only one was concealed from nearby security cams. He tugged on the small metal handle, surprised when the door slid open.

He examined the lock. A thin piece of metal sheeting was secured over the mechanism. The killer was already here, and he had a plan.

Mercer reached for his weapon and took a careful step inside. The side door opened into a maintenance closet which housed an outdated furnace. The derelict contraption had been used to burn refuse and provide warmth before modern technology replaced it with a more efficient and eco-friendly alternative. It remained a rusted heap in the center of the room.

Mercer checked every nook and cranny, but the killer wasn't here. However, the unlocked door meant the killer already gained access to the building and was somewhere inside.

Opening the only other door, Mercer peered around the corner. The hallway was brightly lit. No one was in sight, so he holstered his weapon and made his way down the corridor.

He needed to determine the lay of the land. Once he did, he could figure out what the killer planned. A narrow corridor ended in the lobby. The security checkpoint was to the right. Mercer watched people move seamlessly through metal detectors. Deciding not to waste time, he crossed to the closest guard.

"Excuse me. Has anyone emerged from the hallway besides me?" Mercer pointed. The guard shrugged, unable to supply an answer. "The exterior door to the maintenance room isn't secured. It needs to be fixed immediately."

"Right away, sir." The guard turned to one of his colleagues to relay the information before glancing back at Mercer. "Who are you?"

"Julian Mercer. I'm assisting DCI Yancy." Mercer made a show of looking around. "You didn't happen to notice where he's gotten to."

The guard jerked his chin toward a staircase. "He's in his meeting."

"Thanks, mate."

Jogging up the steps, Mercer searched for signs of an unwanted intruder. The few people in the hallway appeared to be assistants and aides. He moved from room to room, seeing men and women working inside their offices. When he failed to find any indication of the killer's presence, he considered other possibilities. This could be an elaborate ruse, designed to ensnare or frame him for another crime. Before Mercer could give these possibilities further consideration, the fire alarm blared.

"Bollocks." He was too late. He listened to the evacuation protocols over the intercom. If an IED was somewhere inside the building, he didn't have long to find it. The bomb disposal unit must have missed it, or it came in after they performed their sweep. Once everyone was cleared from the building, the bomb squad would perform another check, but they didn't have that kind of time to waste.

The killer had, at most, a five minute head start. Since Mercer didn't spot the bastard in the obvious places, the killer must have entered the building and left almost immediately. If he planted a bomb, it had to be in the maintenance room, and since that was the nerve center of the building, a properly placed charge could take down the entire structure.

Mercer pushed his way through the growing throng, hoping his hasty assessment was accurate. If he was wrong, the crowd exiting the front doors could be marching to its death. *Dammit, think.* If Mercer wanted to make a statement, it would be loud and unforgettable. The problem was the security specialist didn't know what the killer's endgame was. Was this another taunt or revenge on the task force?

The first thing Mercer noticed when he returned to the maintenance closet was the guard he alerted. The man was slumped on the ground, one hand pressed against his throat, the other near his dropped cell phone. The musty air was tinged with the scent of copper. The dark red oozing from between the guard's fingers was a clear indication of what happened.

Mercer drew his weapon and glanced around. As soon as he was positive it was clear, he knelt beside the guard. "Take it easy. You'll be okay." He looked down at the phone, seeing it was connected to emergency services. "Help is right outside. They'll be here any second. Just hang on."

The guard made a gurgling sound and pointed at the furnace. Mercer's gaze darted to the contraption. Then he ripped one of the sleeves off the guard's shirt and wrapped it tightly around the wound. He knew medics wouldn't be allowed into the building until it was swept.

"Press down hard. I'll get you out of here." Mercer placed the guard's free hand over the improvised bandage before removing his own palm. "Did you see him? Did he say anything? Where did he go?"

"He was outside. He heard me and came back in." The gurgling grew worse, and Mercer shushed him.

"Did he go back out?"

The guard nodded.

Mercer went to the doorway with his gun in hand. He kicked open the door and aimed. Pressing himself against the reinforced metal doorjamb, he turned to his right, then his left. The street was clear. The police roped the building off from all sides.

"Okay, hold on." Mercer slipped his hands beneath the guard's armpits and dragged him out of the building. He pulled the man into the street and yelled for help.

Within moments, several uniformed officers surrounded them. The guard was fading fast. Mercer needed him to make it. He was the only person who could identify the killer.

"What did he look like?"

The guard struggled to stay conscious, pointing at the building. "Bomb."

"What did he say?" an officer asked, but Mercer wasn't wasting any more time.

He raced back inside. The guard said there was a bomb, and there was only one place it could be. Mercer carefully opened the rusted door to the furnace. Inside was an IED. Unlike the others, which were versions of pipe bombs, this was different.

The brick of C4 sat in the middle of the furnace. The detonator was on a timer, which was counting down from twenty-four seconds. The blasting cap was buried somewhere in the brick. The wires were tangled and intentionally confusing.

Nineteen seconds.

The furnace might dampen the effects of the explosion, or the ancient rusted metal would blow apart like shrapnel, hitting whatever lines existed, potentially even the gas lines, torching the entire building.

Twelve seconds.

Carefully, Mercer turned the device to the side and examined the crisscrossed wires. He needed to cut one to stop the timer, but he didn't know which. And he didn't have time to figure it out. Remembering a move Bastian pulled during a particularly close call several years ago, Mercer took a deep breath. If he was wrong, it wouldn't matter. None of this would matter.

Seven seconds.

Forcing his hands to steady, he gently tugged at the tip of the wires, sliding the blasting cap through the explosive putty. As soon as the edge was visible, he pulled it clear, doing his best to keep it level. He had to get it away from the C4 or else it would all be for nought, but the wires were still connected and tangled.

Two seconds.

He tossed it into the hallway, pulling the wires free at the exact same moment.

NINETEEN

The blasting cap popped off. And Mercer took a moment to breathe. He didn't like IEDs, explosives, or other incendiary devices. Unfortunately, weapons like that were common in warzones. If it hadn't been for his training, he wouldn't have known what to do.

The killer wanted to make a lasting impression, and Mercer thwarted it. If he hurried, he might catch the bastard before he could escape again. Bursting out the exterior exit as officers from outside rushed toward him and bomb experts entered the maintenance room from the interior entryway, he pushed his way outside.

"The guard?" he asked.

"On his way to the hospital," a cop said. "Who are you?"

"Special ops, assisting DCI Yancy." Mercer sensed he was moments away from being detained. It might have been a lie, but it was close enough to the truth that it might pan out should someone bother to check. "Out of the way. I have to get to Yancy."

"Sir," the officer called after him.

He pointed at the parking garage. "Shut down that structure. Roadblocks at all the openings. No one in or out."

After maneuvering around the barricade, Mercer broke into a run. He pushed his way through the crowd as he searched for the killer. With only the vaguest idea of what the man looked like, he hoped he would intuit whoever stuck out. His only other hope was to find Yancy on the off chance the killer was dead set on eliminating him. If Mercer got to Yancy first, it would increase his chances of finding the killer and ending this.

He pushed through the cluster of people exiting from the front of the building. Fifty or sixty congregated across the street as authorities waved them farther away from the building. The pop from the blasting cap caused quite a stir, and believing it was the first of what would be a much larger explosion, the authorities wanted to clear the area. The two adjacent buildings were also being evacuated.

Mercer spotted someone waiting across the street at the very end of the fray. The man studied his watch. His gaze shifted to the building, and for the briefest moment, he locked eyes with Mercer. The killer's eyes were a muddy brown, carved into chiseled Roman features and topped with short-cropped, dirty blond hair. The man waited for Mercer to recognize him before tucking his hands into his pockets and shuffling away, getting lost in the sea of people.

"Son of a bitch." Mercer tried to push his way through the uncooperative, slow-moving group, feeling the killer getting farther and farther away as each second ticked by. Finally, he shouted, "Gun." His booming voice carried over the commotion, and the crowd dispersed like shrapnel from a grenade.

The police reached for their weapons. Most civilians ducked or scurried in a panic. But the killer was trained. He knew to take cover, but he didn't run and hide.

Through the chaos, Mercer focused on the one man who behaved differently. As soon as he realized his mistake, the killer broke into a run, pushing people out of his way. Several fell to the ground, and more screams erupted. It was bedlam. In the panicked frenzy, someone could be trampled. The police attempted to reestablish control, and Mercer used that opportunity to chase the suspect.

He followed in the killer's wake, closing the distance as the killer desperately zigzagged through the crowd, hoping to break free of the congestion and make a run for it. The area was too mobbed to risk a firefight, so Mercer ran as fast as he could. This arsehole would not escape again.

Half a block later, the killer darted down an alleyway with Mercer on his heels. The killer accelerated, launching himself against the wall and pushing off with the ball of his foot as soon as he made contact with the brick. He grabbed the bottom rung of some scaffolding and pulled himself up, hoping to find a vertical escape route.

Mercer remained a step behind, following the bomber's movements and landing hard on the metal rungs. The killer made it to the level above. The predator and prey continued to move vertically until they reached the roof.

Mercer made it to the top a second later. He rolled to the side as a bullet tore past, mere centimeters from his head. Before he could draw his weapon, the killer was on top of him. Mercer grabbed the barrel and turned it skyward as the killer squeezed off another two shots.

Mercer twisted the man's arm around, sliding his leg across the man's torso to flip their positions, but the killer had gone through the same training. He spun around to prevent the hold, and Mercer locked the killer's wrist in a death grip. The gun fell from the killer's hand, but he swept his body around, freeing himself from the hold.

The two men got to their feet at the same time. The killer had a blade in his left and slashed at Mercer. Mercer spun, elbowing him in the jaw, and unholstered his weapon. By the time he finished the revolution, the killer had wrapped one arm around Mercer's, isolating his shoulder joint and forcing his gun hand out to the side. With his free hand, the killer moved to stab Mercer beneath the ribs. Mercer parried with his forearm. The blade slashed across his arm, ripping the sleeve of his jacket, but that didn't stop Mercer from trying to flip the bastard.

The killer forced Mercer's shoulder up while tugging down on his overextended elbow. Mercer flinched, and the gun fell from his hand. Mercer twisted around again. The two men locked in a deadly dance. With both hands free, Mercer focused on keeping the swinging blade from burying itself in his skin. He miscalculated several times, feeling the sharp edge slice through him over and over. They weren't deep cuts. The killer was playing with him.

Finally, Mercer isolated the knife and headbutted his attacker. The knife slipped from the killer's grip, and Mercer caught the handle in mid-air while wrapping his other arm around the killer's neck in a compromised chokehold. But since Mercer's attention was focused on gaining control of the weapon, the killer elbowed him in the stomach and slipped out of his grasp.

The two rose to their full heights, circling one

another, the discarded firearms only meters away. Mercer knew this man, even if his appearance was slightly different.

"Thomas," Mercer hissed.

"Julian," Thomas Vogel replied, the amusement as evident as the loathing. "I was afraid you lost a step."

"You lost your bloody mind." Mercer lunged forward with the knife.

Vogel sidestepped as the knife ripped his coat to shreds. "Now, now, is that any way to treat your mate? Would you do the same to Bastian? Or Hans?"

Mercer huffed, his vision clouding with red. He would tear this bastard limb from limb. "You're a snake. I'll cut your bleeding head off."

Mercer gripped the knife tighter and barreled into Vogel. Vogel tried to remain standing, but the force of the assault was too powerful. Vogel lost his footing and skidded backward. Instead of leaning forward to correct the imbalance, he threw himself backward, letting the force of Mercer's momentum propel them to the ground. Vogel shoved Mercer over the top of him. Mercer flipped over, coming up in a crouch. He turned, just as Vogel grabbed one of the guns off the ground.

The sight of the firearm did nothing to deter Mercer's resolve as he rushed Vogel again. This time, Mercer rammed his shoulder into the other man's stomach and shoved the blade into Vogel's side. The force of the impact sent the two careening over the side of the roof. They crashed into the scaffolding. It creaked loudly in protest, but Mercer ignored it as he pounded his fists into Vogel's face. The rage consumed him, making him unaware of the outside world.

The sudden pain in his thigh made Mercer blink back to reality. He looked down to find the handle of the knife sticking out of his leg. That sight only fueled his anger, as visions of Michelle flooded over him. He grabbed Vogel by the shoulders and slammed him against the railing. The metal shrieked again, and the scaffolding shifted to the side.

In what felt like slow motion, the fasteners holding it against the wall began to pull away. The scaffolding lurched sideways, and the men crashed against the railing. Their combined weight hastened the collapse, and the cascade continued until they tumbled to the ground amid the tangled metal frame.

Dazed, Mercer climbed to his hands and knees. He struggled to crawl out of the mess, the knife embedded in his outer thigh. He ripped it out, intent on showing Vogel exactly how much pain a blade could inflict.

Mercer had only been pinned for a second, but in that time, Vogel found one of their discarded handguns lying in the street. He picked it up and aimed at Mercer.

"Didn't they teach you not to bring a knife to a gunfight?" Vogel asked, his words coming out breathy. He was wounded from the fight and the fall, but Mercer couldn't tell the extent of his adversary's injuries. "It's a shame this has to end so quickly."

"We'll see." Mercer shifted his grip and threw the knife. The blade buried itself in Vogel's chest, to the left of his heart.

Vogel squeezed off a couple of shots in anger, but Mercer dove out of the way. The killer was losing control. Or he might be losing his grip on consciousness or sanity. Both seemed plausible.

From behind Vogel, two police officers entered the area, their guns trained on the killer. Mercer cursed. This situation would not end well.

"Hands in the air," one of the cops ordered. "Both

of you."

"He's the bomber." Mercer held one hand against his thigh.

Vogel kept his back to the police as he pulled the knife from his chest and dropped it to the ground. "Do you think that was wise, Julian? Involving the coppers is asking for trouble. If you wanted revenge, you should have come for me yourself instead of being a sniveling, pathetic git. And to think, they considered you one of the best. They sent you to save me. Now who needs saving?"

Before Mercer could say a word, Vogel spun. His aim was precise, unlike the way it had been when he fired at Mercer. He took both officers out in a second. They didn't even have time to move their fingers over the trigger before the bullets impacted with their brains.

"I'll be seeing you, Jules," Vogel taunted, racing down the street as more police officers came up behind Mercer.

Mercer gave chase. He wouldn't tolerate letting the killer slip away again. At the end of the alley, Vogel jumped onto a motorcycle. Despite the pain in his leg, Mercer ran as fast as he could. His fingers latched onto Vogel's tattered coat as the killer revved the bike and took off. Vogel jerked at Mercer's hold, but the coat ripped away. And the killer escaped into traffic.

Mercer let out an angry scream, dropping to his knees. He failed. And Vogel's kills increased by two, possibly more. How could an operative turn into nothing more than a cold-blooded psychopath?

"Mercer," Yancy said, catching up to the security specialist, "we'll get him." The detective spoke into the radio, relaying the pertinent information concerning the bomber and his mode of transport. He tucked the radio into his pocket while Mercer climbed to his feet.

"You should sit down."

Mercer looked down at his bloody palm and trouser leg. He didn't even notice the sting. He had to speak to Bastian. They needed to prepare. This was just the beginning.

"The guard," Mercer asked, "did he make it?"

Yancy swallowed and looked away. "No."

Mercer nudged his chin in the direction of the retreating motorcycle. "Neither will he."

"Do you know who he is?"

"Thomas Vogel."

TWENTY

"I didn't have any luck tracking him," Bastian said. "He ditched the bike at the closest Tube station."

"He thinks like we do. Mass transit is the easiest way to disappear. With the various lines, stations, and connections, it'll be blooming impossible to track him." Mercer slammed his fist on the tabletop. "Where is he hiding?"

Bastian clicked a few keys. "As far as Her Majesty is concerned, Thomas Vogel is MIA. His team went out on a recovery, and Vogel disappeared. I'm not certain that was his own doing. Three other members of his team are also considered MIA."

"You think someone's running them?"

"They are properly trained. It could be a rogue faction, or someone's using them for black ops."

"An assassination squad."

"Or a team of hitmen at Her Majesty's service."

"Like I said, an assassination squad. Unless he's operating alone."

"I don't know, but if someone is running him, his

handler doesn't want it to trace back to him. The entire op would be top secret, classified missions with plausible deniability and disavowing anyone who gets caught. The usual guidelines."

Mercer's eye twitched. He let that murdering piece of shit escape. It took all his self-control not to put his fist through the wall. His hands shook as he wrapped the wound on his leg. "Was Vogel acting alone when he killed my wife?"

"I'll keep digging."

Mercer nodded, too irate to speak. He stormed across the room, unable to remain still. He had to keep moving. If he stopped, he'd combust. He flexed the muscles in his arms and chest, trying to work out the anxious energy and rage. Finally, he unclenched his jaw. "How could I have been so blind?"

"Jules—"

"I should have calculated his next move. He never should have gotten off that roof. If I had shot him, it would be over now." The desire to make the traitorous snake suffer was the reason the fight dragged on as long as it did. Maybe Mercer could have ended it sooner.

"That's nonsense. You lodged a knife in his chest and he kept going. He must have had armor or a vest. Shooting him wouldn't have ended this. In case you don't remember, he went through training, just like we did. He knows all the tricks. He was at the top of his class."

"I was better." Mercer scowled, wondering if that remained true and if that wasn't the sole reason Michelle was dead.

"Jules—"

"Enough. Figure out how many of these killers we are dealing with, and find Vogel. He's been killing throughout London. He has to have a base camp.

Until now, he wasn't being hunted. No one knew a bloody thing about what he was doing. He would have let his guard down."

"Like we did?"

Mercer punched through the drywall. His knuckles bled, but he didn't care. "I won't make that mistake again. Vogel knows I'm coming for him and I won't stop."

"Do you think he'll go to ground?"

"No, he'll escalate."

"He intends to torture you. Dragging this out is getting him off. We'll take precautions. MI5 and New Scotland Yard are doing everything they can."

"Someone on the inside is working with him. The mole will cover his tracks and Vogel's."

"I'll stick with the database comparison. We know the police databases were compromised. Either Vogel did it or someone did it for him. Whatever data was altered must be important. Once I pinpoint it, we'll know more."

"In the meantime, a killer or a team of killers is running amok with bricks of C4 and special ops training. Let me know as soon as you have something."

"Where are you going?" Bas asked. "You're wounded. You shouldn't be alone right now."

"I won't be."

"What does that mean?"

"It means I need to keep eyes on his targets. Because of me, the bomb was a failure." Mercer thought of the guard who he sent to his death and the two dead bobbies in the alleyway. "Thomas will try again, and he'll be even more determined not to miss a second time. Watch yourself, Bas. He has an axe to grind. And make sure Hans isn't alone. He called you both out by name."

*   *   *

Mercer blinked his eyes open. His head was starting to bob. He took a deep breath and stretched. If he wasn't sitting inside a car, he would move around to get the blood flowing. He couldn't afford to fall asleep, but being exhausted could prove just as detrimental. He gave the cottage another glance and wondered how Yancy could sleep soundly at a time like this.

London was under siege by the men trained to protect it. Special operatives learned how to handle all kinds of weapons and explosives, what to do in volatile situations, and how to complete a mission. Thomas Vogel had yet to complete his mission, and he wouldn't stop until the job was done. No one was safe. Vogel was unstable, making identifying his targets difficult. The only thing Mercer knew for certain was Vogel set his sights on him and his teammates. He just didn't know why.

Until he learned the killer's identity, Mercer never regretted saving a life, but now, more than anything, he wished he let Thomas Vogel die as a prisoner of war. Vogel was never part of Mercer's team, but their units worked some of the same missions. When Vogel's team was captured, Mercer and his men were tasked with the recovery.

When Mercer moved into the enemy stronghold, several insurgents were already dead, as was half of Vogel's unit. By the time they located Vogel and his remaining teammates, the men were in desperate need of medical attention. Two perished before they made it to the border for an emergency evac.

Mercer remembered the firefight that ensued during the escape. He still had the scars. But at the time, he thought it was worth it. Now he loathed the notion, wishing he put a bullet in Vogel's head years ago.

Mercer never found out exactly what happened at that camp, or why several insurgents were already dead when they arrived. Perhaps that should have been the first indication of how ruthless and deadly Vogel was. Then again, that was true of all operatives. Mercer and his team were no exception. But Mercer couldn't stop himself from looking for some indication of the monster he once fought beside.

"I should have seen it." Since going home, he'd taken to speaking to his wife out loud. "Something was always off about him. He liked the training, particularly hand to hand combat. He always went hard. He put several men in the infirmary with dislocations. It never mattered if they tapped out. He didn't care. He liked to inflict pain, but the instructors saw it as perseverance or gumption. They encouraged him to push everyone's bloody limits instead of acknowledging he was a fucking sadist." He snorted. "You told me once he was damaged goods. I should have listened, paid more attention. I'm sorry, my love. I am so sorry."

He looked around. One of Yancy's neighbors was out of town, so Mercer was using his parking space to conduct surveillance. Bastian was keeping an eye on Lucie's Tavern, but since Yancy was concerned for his daughter's safety, the DCI had taken to visiting the establishment every evening.

Mercer wondered why he didn't show the same type of fierce fatherly love toward the rest of his children, but he wasn't going to inquire. The more people Yancy showed a vested interest in, the more targets Vogel would have. It was best to keep these matters limited.

When the sun came up, Mercer reached for his

phone. "Donovan, are you in position?"

"Affirmative. Get some sleep."

Mercer turned the key in the ignition. He didn't spot Donovan, but he knew the sniper was close. He trusted his teammates. They were his family now. Perhaps they always were.

Hans was aware of the situation and itching to help, but with his recovering shoulder, he couldn't fire a long gun and had an obvious impairment in a physical fight. Still, the reconnaissance expert insisted on being left alone long enough for Mercer to get some rest. Most days, it was only three or four hours, but even that short time span could prove fatal. Vogel could infiltrate the Bauer residence, take out Hans and Perdita, Hans' mum, and be back in hiding before anyone was the wiser.

The team needed to remain vigilant and focused, but they were running themselves ragged. They needed to determine where Vogel was hiding and who was assisting him. Then they'd be able to take down the killer.

A week had passed since the encounter on the rooftop. No real progress had been made. Vogel would strike again soon. Mercer could feel it.

TWENTY-ONE

"I have news concerning the corrupted files recovered from the Met's database," Bastian said into the phone. "Is it okay to discuss these matters now?"

Mercer glanced around. He was tailing Yancy as the detective went about his duties. "Go ahead."

"Right, well," Bastian finished crunching on whatever snack he had before continuing, "two things really. First, I believe I know what was removed from the police notebooks. I found an altered document buried in the databases. It must have been rewritten four times over."

"Out with it."

"Six foot one, dirty blond hair, dark trousers, olive green shirt, combat boots, dark brown eyes, and a full beard. He was unfamiliar to the neighborhood, seemed to appear out of nowhere. Loitered about, made an excuse that he was lawn maintenance and was evaluating the shrubbery. Fifteen minutes later, he was spotted again, moving at a swift pace out of the neighborhood. The eyewitness believed he looked like he might be active military."

"Vogel. Did someone see him enter my house?"

"It doesn't say, but the witness saw Vogel in the area. It should have been investigated further, but it was buried. No real indication how, but based on the various tweaks made to the report, someone went back and changed the reported hair color and deleted a few details so you would fit the bill."

"The coppers."

"Maybe just one. It's too soon to say for certain."

Mercer thought for a moment. Most teams had someone trained to work the computers, hack the security, and bypass cameras. Vogel could have gotten one of his mates to do it for him, or he might have threatened and forced Farnsworth to change his report. "Do you think Vogel realized he was compromised?"

"Jules, every time one of our ops has gone tits up, didn't you know we were compromised from the get-go?"

"Fair point." Before Bastian could get to his second revelation, Mercer caught the briefest whiff of a clove cigarette. "Tell me the rest later." Tucking the phone away, he removed his gun from its holster. He wouldn't be unprepared a second time.

At the present, Yancy was investigating a homicide near one of the embassies. Since the victim was part of a diplomatic security team, London was making certain to send high-ranked officials to take control of the scene. Now that Mercer knew Vogel was close, he didn't believe the murder was a random act of violence or an unrelated incident. Vogel conducted the hit, possibly in fulfillment of Her Majesty's wishes or his own twisted desires.

Mercer moved from shop to shop, taking his time to browse the windows and enter a few establishments. The embassy details and government authorities were out in force to contain the scene and detain anyone they deemed suspicious. Even Yancy didn't appreciate Mercer following him so closely. The DCI believed he could protect himself, and Mercer was positive Vogel would prove the detective wrong if given the opportunity. Thomas Vogel was tying up loose ends and taunting Mercer. Performing a strike against Yancy would kill two birds with one stone.

He's here, Mercer thought. He could smell the terrible cigarettes. Vogel was too much of a professional to light-up while on a mission, but the scent permeated his clothing and skin. The strong odor meant Vogel was close. Too close.

Stepping away from the window, Mercer turned to get a better look around. Utilizing reflections was great when conducting surveillance or recon, but now that he knew the target was nearby, spooking Vogel was no longer a concern. Finding and stopping him were the only objectives.

Chauffeured cars, along with lead and follow vehicles, cluttered the streets. The sidewalks were full of everyone from tourists to government officials. A Tube station was a few blocks to the north, and a bus stop was within view. Mercer watched the people, trying to determine how he would commit a murder in the middle of a busy street.

"Bastard likes his knives." Mercer crossed the street, glancing in Yancy's direction. A large crowd exited the Tube and approached the roped off area from the other side of the street. Someone slipped into the group from a nearby shop. Mercer watched the dark clothing get lost in the sea of people.

Vogel was on the move. He was heading right for Yancy. Mercer moved quickly and carefully, maneuvering around people in the hopes of not causing a scene. He didn't know if Vogel knew he was there, but he wanted to conceal his presence until the last possible moment.

While he continued on a collision course with the killer, Mercer dialed Yancy. "Vogel's here. He's moving toward you."

"What?" Yancy spun, looking in both directions. "Where are you?"

"It doesn't matter." Mercer disconnected, wondering if Yancy would be smart enough to take cover, but the detective moved closer to the sidewalk to wait for the killer. "Knob-end."

Suddenly, someone screamed, and the crowd scattered. A member of the crowd stumbled and hit the pavement. The light reflecting off the blade caught Mercer's eye before the dark clothing and dirty blond hair did. *Vogel.*

Mercer burst into a run, drawing his weapon. The killer stabbed an innocent bystander to create a diversion and was now moving along the outer edge of the group, closing the gap between him and DCI Yancy.

The copper behaved the same as most law enforcement officials. He drew his weapon, scanned the vicinity for signs of danger, and made his way to the victim. Several others followed close behind, radioing for assistance and requesting uniforms establish a perimeter.

"We have another victim. The attacker never left the area. Assume he's armed and dangerous," an officer said into her radio.

Vogel was a master at his craft. He knew how to blend into his surroundings. Mercer broke through the crowd. Spotting the knife, he reached out to grab the weapon, but Vogel pulled back, pocketing the blade and disappearing into the mass, as if he were nothing but an apparition. The police were already boxing in the crowd, but Vogel slipped away.

"Not again." Mercer detoured away from the cluster of people.

Vogel took a sharp right, slipping into a nearby garden. Mercer followed. Vogel didn't make a run for it. Instead, the killer grew more brazen. He greeted a woman he passed. She smiled, and he stopped directly behind her. Slowly, he turned and gave Mercer a wicked grin.

Sensing what was about to happen, Mercer yelled at the woman, "Run."

She turned to see the blade in Vogel's hand. She let out a deafening scream and tried to scramble away, but Vogel grabbed her and pulled her in front of him.

He smiled, holding the tip of the knife against the woman's carotid artery while he sniffed her hair. "This brings back such fine memories."

"Unhand her." Mercer held his gun steady. He could kill Vogel, but the blade was already drawing blood. If the killer twitched, he'd pierce her carotid. The safest shot would be to the brain stem, but Mercer didn't have the proper angle. "She's no one."

"Meaningless, you say?" Vogel nuzzled her neck. "You know what you have to do, Julian." Vogel swiveled, placing himself behind the woman. "You can end this right now. One shot. Aren't you supposed to be the best? Weren't you considered the bloody hero that day?"

"I'm no hero."

"No kidding. Heroes don't take credit for other people's work." Vogel let out an ugly laugh. "I know what you desire. You want to kill me, but you can't."

Mercer took half a step to the left. Vogel moved just as quickly, making a clean shot impossible. "You're a coward. If you want to have this out, let her go. It'll just be you and me," Mercer said, his voice steady even though he felt far from calm.

"I much prefer a threesome. Always have. That's something Hans and I have in common. How is your man these days? Does he still have ten fingers and ten toes?"

"Let. Her. Go." Mercer could barely see straight. He couldn't let Vogel continue to push his buttons.

"Make me."

The woman let out a frantic half-sob, half-scream. And Vogel leaned closer, pressing his lips against her ear and shushing her. Her eyes sought out Mercer's. He knew that look. He'd seen it so many times before. Her silent pleas brought Mercer out of the depths of his need for revenge and back to the present and the reality before him.

"What do you want, Thomas?"

"Is this how you conduct your little negotiations? Is anyone stupid enough to fall for your rubbish?"

"Let her go." Mercer considered other alternatives, but even if his shot only wounded the hostage, Vogel's knife would kill her.

"Negotiate, Julian. You want me to let her go, so you have to give me something in return."

"What do you want?"

"Unload your weapon and throw it away." When Mercer failed to comply, Vogel dug the blade in deeper. "Scream," he whispered, licking her earlobe.

The woman let out a pained, terrified yelp, and Mercer took a step back. "I'm taking my finger off the trigger. Now take the pressure off her neck."

"And now we have a proper negotiation." Vogel waited for Mercer to hold his gun out to the side before he stopped piercing her flesh. "Don't even think about it. No one's that fast."

Mercer forced air into his lungs, realizing he'd been

holding his breath. "What do you want?"

"Throw your gun away."

"No."

Vogel increased the pressure again, and a second rivulet of blood ran down the woman's neck. "Negotiate."

"Okay." Mercer had handled hostage negotiations under worse circumstances, but he couldn't be dispassionate with the man who murdered his wife. "I'll drop my gun if you lose the knife."

"That's more like it. But no. Without the knife and the threat of having another woman's death on your head, I have no leverage. So lose the gun, and I'll let her live. Is this too complicated a concept for you? Let me make it easier. Drop the gun now, or I kill her."

"If you kill her, there's nothing stopping me from killing you. And you know it."

"Do I?"

Mercer didn't like the question. Vogel was insane. Whatever he was considering would only prove how crazy he was. "Okay, I'll do it." Mercer dropped the gun and kicked it away. "This is between us. Let's settle it like men."

"We will, just not today." Vogel shoved the hostage forward, sending her toppling into Mercer.

She screamed, clinging to Mercer like he was her savior. By the time he was able to settle her onto the ground and collect his gun, Vogel was no longer in sight. The woman sobbed, gripping Mercer's leg like a toddler.

Mercer ripped his leg free and raced in the direction Vogel had gone. As Mercer neared the garden exit, he spotted Vogel disappearing down the steps to the Tube.

"Thomas," Mercer shouted.

Vogel turned, gave a tiny salute, and hastened his

retreat.

Mercer chased after him, pushing past the people on the escalator. Vogel jumped the turnstile and darted across the platform. As the train doors closed, the killer slipped inside.

Mercer attempted to pry the doors open, but they wouldn't budge. Vogel remained on the other side of the glass, mere centimeters away. The train started to move, and Mercer fired.

The bullet pierced the small window in the door, but since the train had already gained speed, he had no way of knowing if he hit his target. He needed to stop the train or have it detained at the next stop. Vogel would not escape again. With any luck, the bastard was dead.

Hurrying to get above ground, Mercer sprinted back to the secondary crime scene. The police could mobilize units in seconds. They could commandeer the train and detain its passengers but only if they acted swiftly. Perhaps Yancy was good for something after all.

While Yancy made arrangements to stop the train. Mercer dialed Bastian and gave him an update. They had to locate Vogel before he disappeared again.

TWENTY-TWO

"Search every car. No one in or out," Yancy ordered. The London police had shut down the next Tube station. Everyone waiting for a train was evacuated, and the transit lines were manipulated so no other trains would stop there. The occupants inside the suspect train were being cleared by tactical units. "Separate the men. Thomas Vogel might have changed his appearance."

Mercer watched as the passengers were led off the train and placed in a line along the platform. "He's not here."

"Get onboard and find him," Yancy snapped.

Mercer gave the police officers a wary look and boarded the train. He started at one end and went from car to car, checking every possible hiding spot, no matter how unlikely. When he spotted the broken glass, he knew he was in the right car, but there was no sign of Vogel. From the lack of blood, it was unlikely the killer had been wounded and even less likely he was dead.

"Bollocks," Mercer cursed. Yancy stood beside him, surveying the damage. "Don't."

"What? Mention again what a lousy shot you are?"

"I am not."

"Evidence says otherwise. So far, you're oh for two."

Mercer searched high and low for any indication of where Vogel went or how he escaped. He checked the floor for possible hatches. This was the last connected car. There had to be a way off.

"Argus, you need to hear this," someone said.

"I'll be right back. If you figure out where he went, tell me so I can send actual sharpshooters to take care of him."

"Piss off." Mercer went to the end of the car. Looking through the rear, he saw an exit, possibly for emergencies or maybe maintenance. Either way, it was sealed tight. There was no way Vogel used it to get off the train.

Blowing out a breath, Mercer went back to the broken window. When he fired, the bullet punched a single hole in the glass. Perhaps the force of the wind due to the train's speed made the broken window implode. Glass bits covered the ground. Jagged edges clung to the frame. However, it did provide a rather rudimentary exit.

Mercer leaned out through the opening. The Tube tunnel was rather narrow at times. Jumping out at the wrong time or place would be suicide. But it was the only possible solution, unless Vogel really was a ghost.

Based on the ground glass and the way the jagged edges appeared to be crushed flat in two spots near the bottom, Mercer came to a conclusion. He twisted, surveying the area overhead. He glanced around at the police personnel searching the train, but they weren't paying attention to him.

Grasping the rungs at the exterior, Mercer pulled himself out the broken window. His feet came to rest along the frame. From there, he boosted himself out of the car and to the side. The metal rungs didn't lead any place particularly effective. Mercer looked down at the ground below. Taking care to avoid the third rail, he let go and landed outside the train.

"What the bloody hell are you doing?" Yancy asked, looking down at Mercer from the platform above.

"He jumped the train."

"I believe that refers to getting onto a train, not off. And yes, we know. That's what the lot in the car was saying. The guy's a nutter to attempt something like that." Yancy gave Mercer a pointed look. "Present company included in that assessment."

"He might have doubled back."

"Or he took a maintenance shaft to the surface." Yancy barked orders to his men, radioed for verification that the lines were shut down, and lowered himself to the track below. "Spread out. Consider him armed and dangerous."

"Moscow Rules," Mercer said.

"What?"

"Finger on the trigger." Mercer gave the officers a sideways glance. "Safeties off, gentlemen."

Yancy shrugged. "You heard Mr. Mercer. Do as he says."

Mercer took the torch one of the bobbies handed him and held it beneath his handgun as he headed into the tunnel. With the exception of the occasional maintenance light, everything was dark and eerie. Perfect for an apparition.

Thomas Vogel should have been killed several times over by now. He had close call after close call, but the man was like a cat. He must have nine lives, but Mercer would make sure this one was his last.

Yancy heard something up ahead and signaled to the officers. While the police moved in formation, Mercer slowed his pace. Falling back and retreating were occasionally necessary maneuvers, but they were far from the preferred course of action. If possible, Vogel would have found an alternative escape route, or he had another plan in mind.

He always intended to take the London underground system, Mercer realized. A parallel maintenance hallway ran along the length of the tunnel, walled off and sealed by a locked door. Nothing indicated the door had been tampered with or opened recently, so Mercer moved on. Up ahead, DCI Yancy located Vogel's discarded jacket.

"Any sign of him at the previous station?" Yancy asked into the radio.

Mercer waited for the negative before moving to a wider opening where the tracks split and trains could be rerouted. Knowing the discarded jacket was nothing but a distraction, he killed the torch and continued down the alternate track, following the new line. Roughly a hundred meters in, he saw a maintenance entrance. The door had been jimmied open. Inside was a vertical shaft that led to street level. He climbed the ladder, knowing this was how Vogel escaped.

At the top, Mercer shoved the grate out of the way and poked his head up. Unlike sewer lines, which ran directly beneath heavily trafficked streets, the maintenance shaft let out in the middle of a park. He spotted the gardens in the distance. Vogel didn't go far.

Mercer scanned the area, but he didn't spot the killer. A moment later, someone climbed up the rungs of the ladder. Mercer turned as a police officer emerged, followed closely by DCI Yancy.

"He's gone," Yancy declared, letting out a huff. "We'll find the bastard."

"Only if he wants you to," Mercer said. "Watch yourself. You're his next target."

Without elaborating, Mercer headed in the direction of his parked car. Vogel wouldn't be foolish enough to make another attempt today. He already failed twice. The police were out in force due to the two homicides and obvious threat. The authorities were on high alert, and they knew the killer's identity.

On the windshield, Mercer found a scrap of paper. He plucked it from beneath the wiper and scanned the area.

The negotiation isn't over. I say when it is.

Stuffing the paper in his pocket, Mercer checked the vehicle to make sure it wasn't booby-trapped. Once he was positive it was safe, he unlocked the door. After a thorough scan to make sure Vogel didn't plant a tracker, Mercer glanced around. The killer wasn't close, but he was watching.

After raising two fingers in a v, Mercer slid behind the wheel and slammed the door. He'd ditch the car a few blocks from here, but right now, he had to get moving. Yancy was surrounded by police personnel and knew the threat was real. The DCI would be careful, which meant Vogel might settle for a secondary target, and the only name that came to mind was Hans.

TWENTY-THREE

"Tea, Julian?" Perdita Bauer asked as she placed the tray on the table. "You look tired. Are you hungry? You must be hungry."

"I'm fine, madam," Mercer replied. "Don't go to any trouble on my account."

"No trouble at all."

"This was a mistake." He wanted to speak to Hans, but showing up here might have been precisely what Vogel wanted. If the killer tracked him, he'd know where Hans was. It was bad enough Bastian and Donovan were already coming and going with regular frequency. It would be best to have the Bauers relocated.

Perdita stiffened, folding her arms over her chest and staring at Mercer with an intensity even the most lethal of combatants rarely demonstrated. "Was it a mistake?"

"Yes."

"Really?" Her gaze darted to the hallway. Hans would be finishing his rehab session any moment.

"When my boy joined the military, I wept. When he signed on to the bloody SAS, I was terrified." Her eyes went hard. "Do you remember what you promised me?"

"I would keep him safe." Mercer felt the pit in his stomach.

"That's what you said."

"I know."

"Well, I don't. Hans doesn't blame you, and we both know what a cantankerous git he can be at times." She laughed softly. "What happened?"

"He didn't tell you?"

"I want to hear it from someone else."

"No one else was in position. There was a boy. Hans saved him. It's all he cared about. He had to protect the lad."

She nodded sadly. "He's right. It wasn't your fault. It was mine. Goes back to his brother and the beatings they took as children." Tears welled in her eyes, and she dabbed at them, doing her best not to cry.

Understanding her guilt and regret, Mercer reached for her hand and gave it a tender squeeze. "I won't let anyone hurt him again."

"Hans is a man. He'll do as he pleases." She stood. "I'll get you something to eat."

"I'm fine."

"I don't know about Jules, but I'm feeling a bit peckish. Maybe a few biscuits to tide me over until supper," Hans said as he followed a toned brunette down the hallway. The doctor smiled at Mercer, gave Hans a quick kiss, grabbed her bag from the coat closet, and went out the door. Hans sunk into the chair and let out a contented sigh, his gaze lingering on the front door. "Maggie made sure I worked up quite the appetite. She really put me through the wringer this afternoon." He rubbed his sore shoulder.

"Says I'm making great progress, though. I can be field ready whenever you say the word, Jules."

"Not yet." Mercer poured a second cup of tea from the serving tray and handed it to Hans. "We need to discuss Thomas Vogel."

"Bastian told me. How can I be of service?"

"Vogel's made it a point to mention you during several of our encounters."

"You think he'll target me?" Hans frowned, nodding to himself. "Fucking tosser. Always liked to prey on the weak. Apparently, people don't change. And apparently, he doesn't realize I'm not weak."

"We should move you and your mum to a safe house."

"She'd never allow it. And it's not necessary. You already have Bas and Donnie pulling sentry duty. Frankly, Jules, you need someone with you. Thomas is unpredictable. He's vindictive."

"He killed my wife," Mercer managed through clenched teeth. "He will not take anyone else I care about."

"Why haven't you ended this?"

Mercer put the cup down before he smashed it in his hands. "I don't bloody know."

"Yes, you do." Hans sat up straighter, slipping his arm out of the sling and stretching. "You won't risk this monster endangering another innocent life." He winced and reached for the heating pad. "I can pop a few painkillers, and you and I can make a run at him. We'll put this to bed and be back in time for supper."

Mercer snorted. "Brilliant. Just one snag, we have to locate him first."

Finally, Hans understood the reason for Mercer's visit. "Where's Bas and Donovan?"

"Maintaining eyes on Vogel's other two possible targets."

"And you think since I went through training with him, we have some kind of bond and I know where he might be." Hans thought for a moment. "I know the places he used to hang out. And I have some thought on who might help him, but I don't know how bloody likely any of them are."

"Out with it. We're on a clock."

TWENTY-FOUR

"This is the place?" Mercer asked, eyeing the dilapidated building.

"Used to be. It's been years. It could be a drug den by now," Hans said, opening the car door and stepping out into the cool night air.

"As if it wasn't before." Mercer gave Hans a stern, warning look. "You should wait here."

"Like hell." Hans went down the steps and knocked on the basement door.

Mercer hung back, studying their surroundings for signs of trouble. After a few exchanged words with the bouncer, Hans and Mercer were invited inside. The underground club, as it was, had been one of Vogel's favorite spots. It was an out of the way strip joint, where naked women danced in cages and illegal activities took place in the back rooms.

"Is this the type of establishment you and Donovan disappear to?" Mercer asked.

"You'd think so, but no. We prefer places with more disinfectant and fewer junkies. Less chance of getting knifed in the back, arrested in a raid, or contracting something venereal." Hans made his way to the bar. "Hey, is Pete around?" he asked the bartender.

"Who's asking?"

"Bauer."

The bartender gave him a look. "Aight, mate. I'll check."

Before Mercer could ask any questions, a small, impish fellow stepped out of the back office. He smiled brightly and held out his hand. "Hans, my boy, haven't seen you in years." He shook Hans' hand emphatically, and Mercer watched as the recon expert bit back a wince. "Are you and your mate looking for something in particular? Let me guess, you're on leave."

"Actually," Hans said as Pete signaled for two of the girls to come over, "I was wondering if Vogel's been around lately."

"He's been popping in and out for a time. Why don't you make yourselves comfortable, have some drinks, and enjoy the entertainment? He normally arrives pretty late."

"Right-o," Hans said as one of the topless women ran her hands against his chest.

Pete turned to the bartender. "First round's on the house for Hans and his friend."

Once Hans and Mercer were situated, Mercer dismissed the women with a handful of quid and an annoyed stare. "Now what?" he asked, placing the untouched pint on the table.

"We wait."

Mercer reached for his phone and dialed Bastian. "We might have a lead on Vogel. Hans and I are at an underground club. The owner says Vogel's been here recently." Mercer gave Bastian the address and removed the keys from his pocket. "You need to leave."

"Are you daft?" Hans asked.

"Need I remind you that you are not in any condition to face Vogel?"

"Hate to break it to you, but neither are you. This plonker has you so twisted around you're about to snap. You aren't thinking clearly, and we all know how that affects mission performance."

"This isn't a mission. This is personal. And I don't need your help."

"Pretty sure that's why you came to me mum's house. And it's the only bloody reason you even know about this club." Hans looked around the room. "See that bastard in the corner, hand shoved in his pocket?"

"Aye."

"Don't know that I ever spoke to him, but I recognize him. He's one of Pete's regulars."

"He might know Vogel." Mercer moved to stand, but Hans grabbed his forearm.

"What are you going to do, Jules? Do you even have a plan? It's a risk. A confrontation could tip off Vogel, and like Pete said, the wanker might show up a little later this evening."

"Then we wait."

While they waited for the rest of their team to arrive, Hans spoke at length about the typical places Thomas Vogel frequented. The more he spoke, the more obvious it became that Vogel wasn't quite right. He liked danger and being on the edge. He spent time in places where merely his presence could jeopardize his life and career, and that was what he did with his free time. During training, Vogel went to extremes. He pushed limits and took a few beatings because of it, but it never deterred him. Nothing would deter the psycho from whatever he set his mind to.

"Jules," Hans leaned in close, "I can't tell you how sorry I am. If I had any idea what Thomas was capable of or that he was responsible, I would have told you."

"I know."

Eventually, the rest of the team arrived, much to Mercer's annoyance. But since things were quiet on the other fronts, Donovan and Bastian decided it was best to provide support where the situation might escalate. But as the night dragged on, there was no sign of Vogel.

Mercer was ready to interrogate every person in the club. He'd already spoken extensively to the bartender and several of the dancers.

"You should take Hans home," Donovan said, sidling up to him. "Things might get rough, and he'll throw himself into the middle of the fray. He's already blaming himself for not seeing the connection earlier, and with his injury, he feels like a burden to the team. He doesn't enjoy the constant babysitting. Bringing him here was a bad idea. He'll do something moronic and destroy his chances of ever recovering."

"He wouldn't give me the address otherwise," Mercer said.

"And he won't leave until you do." Donovan glanced back at Bastian. "It's the right call, commander. Bas and I can handle matters here. Vogel isn't showing up tonight. But if we find anything, we'll ring you immediately."

"Fine. We'll check on Yancy and Lucie's pub and call it a night. We don't want that bastard to strike now that we're all here. Care to come along, Hans?" Mercer asked.

"Okay."

TWENTY-FIVE

Mercer shot up in bed. The house creaking as the morning sun forced the building materials to expand was a sound to which he was no longer familiar. He rubbed his eyes and took a deep breath. Four hours, that would have to be a sufficient amount of sleep. He didn't have time to laze around. Vogel remained at large, and until ravens were picking at his carcass, Mercer wouldn't rest.

As he went about his morning ritual, he wondered why the bastard was being so careful. Vogel had been positively reckless with the attempted bombings and brazen enough to phone in the threats to the police. But as soon as he revealed himself, he went back into hiding. Vogel was nothing but a coward. His need for self-preservation outweighed his narcissistic ego, unless he was biding his time in preparation for a massive strike.

That unsettling thought was the one that drove Mercer insane. Vogel knew exactly what buttons to push. It took years to uncover the killer's identity, and now that Mercer had it, he still couldn't act. Vogel had Mercer and his team so consumed with playing defense, they had little time to mount an offensive. That needed to change.

Wiping his face on the hem of his shirt, Mercer moved past the dresser, letting his fingers play against a few of the trinkets before going into the guest bathroom. "I will end this. I will put a stop to his madness. And he will pay for the way he made you suffer, my love."

Prepared for another day, Mercer made sure he had adequate gear. A bullet was too humane, but if that was the only guaranteed way to end it, he would take the shot. However, if he had his way, Vogel's death would be anything but humane. This wasn't about honor or humanity. This was about retribution.

He flipped through the surveillance feeds from the cameras placed around the house before dialing Bastian. "Anything?"

"We found a possible alias. This bloke, William Bishop, never existed prior to eight months ago. He popped into existence right around the time we returned to London. Bishop rents a flat above a grocer, pays in cash, and has no credit cards or bank accounts. He exists off the grid. The kicker is the market was across the street from our flat. That's how he's been keeping an eye on us."

"How'd you find this?"

"Magic," Bastian said, "or several shots of Jager, bribery via a pole dancer, and a gun pressed to our informant's naughty bits."

"Vogel wouldn't remain in one place. William Bishop can't be his alias."

"Maybe not, but there's a connection."

"Misdirect?" Mercer asked.

"Or this Bishop chap is working with Vogel. He

could be providing him with the means necessary to conduct his hits."

"Give me the address."

"Donovan's already there. The flat is vacant. Grocery store's doing a decent business. Donovan spoke at length with the owner. I ran his background. I don't think he's connected."

"We need to make sure."

"I'll text you the address."

Mercer pulled the device from his ear. He had two messages. One from Yancy. "Another thing, Yancy wants to meet. Says he might have something and wants me to swing by Lucie's tonight. Plonker. He's putting his daughter's life in danger by staying so close."

"The damage is already done. Vogel knows about the pub. It's best Yancy keeps watch."

"Does he have units assisting?"

"No. I don't think he trusts his colleagues. He's convinced Vogel has a connection on the inside, and even if he doesn't, Vogel must be tapped into the police systems. It's best he's monitoring Lucie on his own."

"He isn't. We're assisting."

"True, but he doesn't know that, Jules."

"Has Hans made any progress?"

Bastian blew out another breath, and Mercer suspected he was smoking. "I practically had to chain him to bed after you dropped him off last night. He's dying to venture out to Vogel's other haunts, but I wouldn't allow him to leave. Instead, Hans made contact with several of the men who were part of their candidate class. Most haven't spoken to Vogel since they were given their troop assignments. No one knows anything, but that hasn't stopped Hans from digging. He's bored and needs to feel useful."

"He's going to get himself killed."

"Give him some credit. He's smarter than that."

"What about the remaining members of Vogel's troop? Have we spoken to any of them?"

"It's too risky."

"What have you found on your end?" Mercer asked. "If Vogel's still operational, his team should know where he is and what he's doing."

"Those who aren't MIA are part of the Reserve now. They were reassigned after the capture. They've been stateside for a while. I'm working on pinning down the actual paperwork. From the whispers I've heard, they're handling anti-terrorism measures and national security."

"Might explain his recent fascination with explosives. Does he want his own teammates to hunt him as well?"

Bastian went silent, except for some nervous tapping. Finally, he said, "Vogel wants to be stopped. He might not realize it, but that's why he selects the targets he does. He's hurting his own kind because he knows we're the only ones who can stop him. If you don't do it, Jules, he'll keep killing until he finds someone who can."

"He's already dead. He just doesn't know it yet. Keep on this Bishop chap. Let me know what you find. If he's connected to the service, we need to know. I'll rendezvous with Yancy tonight and see what he's found. In the meantime, tell Hans to stay put. Someone needs to be there to protect his mum. That should convince him to listen to reason."

"He might need more."

"Tell him it's a bloody order."

Mercer grabbed his gear and met Donovan outside the grocery store. The tactician already searched the flat above, but Mercer wanted to do it himself. The two went up the stairs and let themselves inside. As Bastian said, the place was vacant. It had been cleaned and wiped.

Kneeling down, Mercer removed the vent cover and searched inside. He'd already checked the built-in cabinets and closets for hidden compartments. "The bastard's been close to us ever since we arrived. He's been watching."

"We had no way of knowing that," Donovan said. "We didn't know we were being hunted."

"I'm being hunted," Mercer corrected. "Seems only fitting since this is the bastard I've been hunting. Did you get a description of Bishop?"

"It's not Vogel." Donovan removed his phone and scrolled through the photos. "That's a copy of his ID. Bastian's already on it."

"The glasses and beard are meant to disguise his features."

"We think he might be one of the men who went MIA. But we can't be certain."

"Keep looking." Mercer replaced the vent cover, finding nothing inside. "Bishop must have been set up here to monitor us."

"Unless Vogel planted the name and the story to keep us off balance and chasing ghosts. It could be misinformation. He knows we're desperate and searching."

"It doesn't matter. One way or another, I will find him."

*   *   *

"We haven't received any tips or threats in days. No suspicious murders have occurred. Unofficially, did you take care of the problem?" Yancy asked. The pair was nestled in the rear corner of the pub.

"Hoping to pin another homicide on me?"

"No, Mr. Mercer, I just want to know if I need to watch my back."

"Thomas Vogel remains on the loose. Your message said you had a lead."

"Potential lead. We've analyzed the materials Vogel used to make the bombs. They're military-grade."

"No surprise."

"The task force is using its resources and connections to figure out how Vogel gained access to the materials. We're working on it, but it'll take time. I hear you might have found something of interest with the data breach."

"Do not concern yourself with the measures I am taking."

"Anyway, we believe we're narrowing down Vogel's location."

"How?" Mercer asked.

"Don't worry yourself over the details. I just wanted to make certain we weren't wasting our time if the threat was eliminated."

"Not yet."

"You realize every bobby in the city is after this guy. He's killed two of our own, two security guards, stabbed a civilian, and attacked that woman, not to mention injuring several with the two detonations. He's escalating, We want to stop him before things get even more out of hand."

"The death toll would have been higher if the third IED wasn't disassembled."

"Thanks for that."

"I don't want your gratitude."

"Well, regardless, you have it." Yancy glanced at Lucie who was slammed with work tonight. "Why are you convinced Vogel will target her?"

"You love her. He knows it."

"That's it?"

"Yes."

"That seems rather alarmist."

"If you're lucky, he'll slaughter you and leave her out of it. But I wasn't that fortunate. I don't know what plans he has for you, but you ought to prepare for the worst. He followed you here on several occasions. He performed reconnaissance. He knows the building's layout and the most efficient way to get inside. He could strike at any moment. You. Her. Someone else. It's what he does."

"How do you know?"

Mercer gave him a look. "It's what I would do."

"This goes back to the task force and the missing pages. Vogel killed Farnsworth because a witness provided a description. Why didn't he kill me then?"

"That's a very good question, indeed." Mercer contemplated it for several moments. "You should disappear and send Lucie away, someplace you don't know about. I would suggest you tell your ex-wife and other children to do the same."

"I would, but they refuse to speak to me." He glanced back at Lucie. "She's all I have left."

"Then do whatever it takes to keep her safe." Something caught Mercer's attention outside, and he stood. "Stay here."

Before Yancy could utter a single word, Mercer was out the door.

TWENTY-SIX

Outside, the darkened streets added to the danger. Mercer removed his gun and buried his hand in his pocket. The last thing he needed was to alarm a pedestrian and trigger a panic. Everyone needed to remain calm and keep to themselves. A repeat of the hysterical woman being taken hostage was unacceptable. If it hadn't been for her and Mercer's vow to protect innocents, he would have taken the shot. Even if the bullet ripped through her, it would have killed Vogel, and a part of him knew that was precisely what the psychopath tried to force him to do. But that was the line Mercer wouldn't cross. It would make things less complicated, but the reason for doing this would lose all meaning.

Mercer trudged down the street, pursuing a man in a dark coat and an ivy cap. The same man passed in front of the bar three times since Yancy entered. Mercer hastened his pace, moving quickly and carefully until he was directly behind the man. The smell of clove cigarettes grew stronger.

Removing the gun from his pocket, Mercer pressed it into the man's back. "Move into the alleyway." The man tried to turn around, but Mercer placed a firm hand against his shoulder. "Move."

Mercer shoved him face first against the brick wall. Carefully, he glanced back onto the street, but he didn't spot any additional threats.

"Take my wallet. I don't have much, but it's yours," an unfamiliar voice said.

Mercer spun the target around, surprised to discover it wasn't Vogel. "Where is he?"

"Who?"

Mercer pressed the barrel of his gun against the man's forehead. "Thomas Vogel. Where is he?"

"I don't know who that is."

"Where did you get the coat? Why are you parading in front of the pub?"

"Some bloke promised me five hundred pounds if I walked up and down the block for the rest of the night. He said it would be a great gag to play on the drunks."

"Show me who said it."

"I don't know where he went." The man pointed to an alcove across the way. "He was over there, beneath the sign."

"Go." Mercer shoved him backward.

Keeping his gun down at his side, Mercer raced back to the pub. His head remained on a swivel. It was a mistake to leave Yancy and Lucie unguarded. Vogel paid the man with the coat and hat to serve as a distraction, and Mercer was stupid enough to fall for it.

A bullet punched into the wall a centimeter from Mercer's head. He dropped to the ground. Another shot hit the front window. The glass shattered, showering him in shards. He heaved himself off the ground and tugged the pub door open, diving inside as another three shots impacted millimeters from his ear.

The sniper fire continued in a deadly spray. Most of Lucie's customers hit the ground the moment bullets started flying. Yancy shouted at the others to seek cover.

Mercer tucked himself against the doorframe and glanced outside as more shots bombarded the bar. The shooter was across the street on a roof. It's how he was getting such sharp angles into the pub.

"Lucie," Yancy said, "where's the piece I gave you?"

"Upstairs. I can get it."

"No, stay down," Yancy insisted, but she remained low behind the bar, making a break for the staircase as another barrage drew to an end.

She was fearless, more so than her father. But she might have been just as foolish.

"Argus," Mercer said, "go. Keep her safe."

Yancy ran for the back of the pub. As a distraction, Mercer fired at the sniper, but at this distance, he had no hope of hitting his target. He needed a scope and a rifle or some way to flank the shooter.

The gunfire focused again on Mercer, and he dove beneath a table, flipping it on its side to provide cover. The pub had a rear exit, but it let out at the side of the building where there was little to no cover. Going out the side door would mean no uncertain death if Vogel was monitoring the surroundings. But Mercer was counting on the shooter being too focused on the front entrance to notice someone slipping out the rear door.

Mercer glanced at the terrified drunks. Most were on their phones with the authorities or calling loved ones. A few grabbed bottles from the bar and gulped down the contents, convinced they had moments left to live.

"You," Mercer said to someone speaking to the police, "tell the coppers a sniper is on the roof across the street. They need to send a tactical unit to dispose of the threat. The rest of you, stay down, and don't move into his line of sight or you're dead."

Mercer crept into the rear hallway. As soon as he was no longer visible from the front, he moved swiftly to the side door. He unlatched it and checked his weapon. Opening the door might be enough to attract Vogel's attention. It would take a second or two for him to reposition the sniper rifle and aim. Mercer was only guaranteed those two seconds. Anything after that was an oversight on Vogel's part.

For the briefest moment, Mercer wished Hans was acting as overwatch or Donovan was providing cover support. Even Bastian, who rarely worked the long guns, would be an asset. But he was alone, and he always knew when it came to facing his wife's killer, he would do it by himself.

As soon as he opened the door, a bullet lodged into the metal door where his head would have been had he stepped out. He stumbled backward. The bastard had a thermal scope. That's how he knew where Mercer would be.

Mercer swore, realizing it also meant Vogel knew where every single person inside the pub was hiding. As he raced back into the front room, he grabbed a phone from the closest person and dialed one of the numbers he memorized. "Vogel's outside Lucie's pub with a rifle and thermals. We're pinned down. The police are on the way. I need an ETA."

Bastian picked up another phone and dialed Donovan. "Get to the pub. Vogel has Jules trapped inside." Then Bastian switched phones. "Jules, can you manage?"

"For now. Vogel will use the police as fodder if we

don't intervene."

"I'm on it. No massacres on my watch, mate."

More bullets whizzed past, and someone cried out in pain. "Stay away from the windows," Mercer said, but no one in the pub had been hurt. "Shite."

Leaping over the bar, he landed in a crouch. The floor was wet and covered in liquor and glass. He went up the steps, taking them two at a time, even as he heard gunfire echoing in the street and bullets impacting against the exterior of the building. The staircase was walled in, but Lucie's flat had several windows facing Vogel's position. Mercer reached the landing and pushed the door open.

Lucie was hunkered down in the hallway. Yancy was clutching his bicep. He aimed out one of the broken windows, and Mercer saw the faintest green dot. He lunged, knocking Yancy to the ground a millisecond before the death shot could be made. The bullet grazed Yancy's temple but wouldn't cause any lasting damage, aside from a nasty scar.

Lucie let out a shriek.

Mercer looked at her from his position on top of her father. "Stay there."

"Argus?" she asked.

Mercer rolled to the side and crouched near the window.

"I'm okay," Yancy said, wiping the blood from the side of his face. He moved to the other side of the window. "How can he fire so quickly?"

"He knows what he's doing, and he came prepared," Mercer said.

"Are you certain he's alone?"

"The muzzle flash is limited to a single location. There's only one active shooter."

"And he can fire like that?" Yancy didn't risk another glance outside. "How can he predict where we are?"

"Thermals." Mercer scanned the room for something that would mask their heat signatures or serve as a distraction.

"What if we crank the thermostat?" Lucie asked.

"It would take too long, even if the windows weren't broken." He edged away from the window and moved into her kitchen. A few bottles of liquor sat atop the counter. "Argus, I need your help."

After assembling two Molotov cocktails, Mercer handed one of the unlit bottles to Yancy. "As soon as I leave the room, I want you to count to ten. Light it. Wait a couple of seconds and drop it out the window. Straight down. Understand?"

"Yes," Yancy said.

"Good man. A tactical team is en route. What is their typical response time?"

"Five to seven minutes. What are you going to do?"

"Make sure no one else gets killed." Mercer nodded at the bottle. "Start counting." He had to act quickly. Once the bottle exploded in front of the pub, the flame would temporarily screw with the thermal imaging. That would give Mercer a brief window to get out the side exit, toss the other bottle to mask his movements, and get across the street before Vogel could reposition his weapon.

Donovan was on the way. Cover fire would make this easier, but regardless, Mercer would make it work. He stopped at the side door and waited. He began counting the same time Yancy did, but he wasn't sure how quickly the detective was counting or even if he could count as high as ten.

A sudden unexpected scream told Mercer the bottle was dropped. He burst out the side door. Simultaneously, he lit the rag and flung the bottle directly into the street.

Before it even hit the ground, he ran as fast as he could. The Molotov cocktail landed, but he kept moving. As soon as he made it safely across the street, he slowed his pace. Vogel was above. Somewhere on the roof of this building. It was two stories with no visible means of exterior roof access. The building was a combination of shop and restaurant, but given the late hour, both were closed.

Since the doors showed no sign of breaking and entering, Vogel must have entered during business hours and remained in hiding until everyone left. Then he set up on the roof and waited.

Bloody hell, how did he know about the meet? Mercer shot off the lock on the security gate and lifted the metal out of the way. He moved to the front entrance. He entered the establishment, finding it strange that no alarms were triggered. Vogel must have disabled them so as not to accidentally alert the authorities of his presence.

After a quick scan for potential hostiles, Mercer went upstairs. The restaurant was on the second level. Roof access was at the rear, past the kitchen. The sudden vibration in his pocket had him searching for a hidden enemy until he realized the source.

"I'm moving into position. What's your location?" Donovan asked.

"Inside the sniper's building, making my way to the roof now." Mercer gave the kitchen a quick glance before moving to the staircase. "If you have a shot, take it."

"Copy that," Donovan replied. "I'm not seeing any movement. Switching to thermals. Bloody hell. The exhaust fan is creating a blooming blind spot. He might be positioned directly in front of the door and in way of the fan. I need to reposition."

"Keep searching. If he's not on this building, scan

the other rooftops. Make sure he didn't jump across."

"Right-o."

Tucking the phone into his pocket, Mercer gripped the gun in both hands and continued down the corridor. Vogel was here. He could practically smell him.

Mercer reached for the doorknob to the roof. He placed his left on the knob and kept his gun at the ready. The sound of police sirens erupted from below. He had to stop Vogel before the bastard killed again.

The moment he tugged the door open, he realized his mistake. Vogel rigged the door with a shaped charge. The reinforced steel door blew clear off its hinges, slamming into Mercer hard enough to knock the breath from his lungs and propel him several meters backward. His back collided with the wall while the door crushed his front.

When he blinked back to consciousness, he was aware of the acrid smell of detonated C4 and the humming throb of pain coursing through his entire body. Slowly, he crawled out from underneath the door. He saw his gun lying on the ground and scooped it up before struggling to get his legs beneath him.

Vogel. It was the singular thought in his mind as he retraced his steps back to the roof, ignoring the layer of soot and the spotty fires that ate sections of the carpet and lapped against the wood fixtures. Even in the dark, Mercer could see the scorch marks on the roof from the bomb's blowback. If Vogel had been near the door, he would have been incinerated, but the killer was too smart to make an amateur mistake like that. The bloody bastard booby-trapped the roof on the off chance someone tried to stop him.

Movement near the far corner caught Mercer's attention. He stepped carefully, watching for additional traps. The tactical unit below heard the explosion and intended to breach. He could hear the chirp of their radios and barked orders, which meant Vogel could hear them too. Hopefully, the distraction would work in Mercer's favor.

The shadow darted around another smokestack. Mercer edged farther to the right, hoping to come up on Vogel from the other side and end this. Donovan was close. As soon as he had a clear shot, he would take it.

Spotting a tripwire, Mercer stopped. His eyes remained on the last spot he saw Vogel, even as he knelt to examine the cord. Carefully, he removed a switchblade from his pocket, flipped it open, and cut the wire. It was a rudimentary pull cord hooked to a grenade.

Mercer was a meter away from the smokestack when a rumble erupted beneath his feet. The ground shook hard enough to knock him over, and then the whole building came crashing down.

TWENTY-SEVEN

Donovan sifted through sections of the roof, finally locating Mercer. "Jules, are you all right?"

Mercer blinked, noting the rubble around him. It was raining, and he looked up at the cloudy night sky. "Where the fuck is he?"

"Buried somewhere in this mess." Donovan held out his hand and helped Mercer up. "You're lucky you were thrown to the side. The roof split, and you were on the downslope. It kept you clear of the collapse." Donovan watched Mercer brush debris and dust off his clothing. He was cut up and bruised. "It looks like Vogel went straight down."

"The police?"

Donovan pressed his lips together and looked away. "From my position, it looked like the device was triggered a minute after they entered."

"He had the door to the roof rigged. He must have booby-trapped the entire building." Mercer tried to think, but it didn't make sense. "Why would he kill himself?"

"I don't think that was his intention. We'll know more when the search team finishes."

"You're absolutely positive he didn't escape?"

"I didn't see anyone get clear before the building came down."

"Did you see him on the roof?"

Donovan shook his head. "I didn't have time to reposition. And the subsequent explosions screwed with the night vision and thermals. He must have had some fancy gear to see through those smokestacks."

"Or he repositioned once he knew I was coming for him." Mercer glanced back at the bar, spotting Yancy getting evaluated by a medic while the DCI barked orders at the tactical team and the detective in charge. "Update Bastian and search the perimeter."

Mercer limped away, circling around to stay off the coppers' radar. Until he knew for certain Vogel was trapped beneath a few tons of concrete and steel, he couldn't risk police interference. He needed to speak to Yancy in private.

Additional units arrived to assess the damage, cordon off the street, and question the barkeeps and customers. Yancy sat in the back of an ambulance, watching the medics evaluate and triage the injured. Lucie was inside the pub, speaking to an inspector while gesturing emphatically at the window and rear staircase.

Mercer crept up to the ambulance and leaned against it. He gave Yancy a sideways glance before returning his attention to the search and rescue teams assessing the collapsed building for survivors.

"How many casualties?"

Yancy looked at him. "Bloody hell. I thought you were dead."

"Not yet."

Yancy jerked his chin across the street. "The breach

triggered an explosion. We won't know more until the bomb squad and fire department get here. Six men breached. They've pulled two out. They were pretty banged up. Worse than you." Yancy looked back at the bar. "Is this over?"

Mercer didn't respond.

"Well?"

"I won't be certain the killer's dead until I spit on his corpse." The fury and rage burned inside, fiercer than before. It was unexpected. Mercer thought he'd feel a sense of calm, relief, or a release once the man who murdered Michelle was no longer breathing, but he didn't feel any of that, which is why he wasn't convinced Vogel was dead.

"He must be. The building crumbled beneath him. No one saw him crawl away."

"I survived, so did two of your colleagues."

"If he lived through it, he must be trapped. We'll dig him up and bury his arse," Yancy vowed.

As the hours dragged on, Mercer felt himself crashing. Through sheer stubbornness, he remained standing, leaning against the side of Lucie's pub as teams dug through the mess.

"They found three sets of remains. They'll have to use dental records or DNA to identify the bodies. Two more coppers were pulled out of the mess. One was dead. The other's getting airlifted to the hospital. It doesn't look good," Donovan said.

Mercer nodded. At least the only injuries inside the pub were cuts and scrapes and one case of alcohol poisoning. He rubbed a hand down his face, wincing when his scraped palm came into contact with the glass shards embedded in his skin. "Do you have a secure line?"

"Here." Donovan handed Mercer his phone.

"Bas, I need you on top of the identifications. Six

coppers entered the building. Four were identified. But the authorities found three sets of yet to be identified remains. I don't care what you have to do, make sure you oversee it. I don't want Vogel's identity to be swept under the rug. If he was killed inside that building, we need to know for certain. Is that clear?"

"Understood."

Mercer handed Donovan back the phone.

"What should we do?" Donovan asked.

"We wait until we're certain the bastard's dead."

Now that the sky brightened in the pre-morning light, Yancy was willing to go to the hospital. The medics were concerned about the graze to his temple, and Lucie was adamant he get checked out.

"Mercer," Yancy called, "a word." Mercer crossed to the ambulance, glaring at the medic who mentioned he looked worse for wear and could also use a check-up. "Give us a moment, please." As soon as the medic left, Yancy said, "I have to get cleared by a doctor before I can return to work, but as soon as I do, I'll make sure identifying the remains is a priority. I'll let you know once we have a name. But I need you to do me a favor. Another favor. I need you to protect Lucie. She can't stay at the pub. It's destroyed. She has nowhere to go. Look after her until this is settled. I'll do anything you say."

"She's an adult. She has her own say in the matter." The team was already stretched thin, but if the threat was gone, it wouldn't hurt to put the woman up in a safe house for a day or two.

"Don't change your tune now. You insisted I keep her safe. The thought of leaving her in jeopardy is unbearable. I can't lose someone I love, Mr. Mercer. I just... I can't go through that again. I'd rather die than risk seeing something happen to her. You of all people should understand that."

"Very well. But you will call with the slightest update."

"Agreed."

Mercer left Yancy in the back of the ambulance and went to speak to Donovan. "Change of plans. We need to move Lucie to a secure location until this matter is resolved."

"We can put her in one of our flats. Security won't be as tight as we're used to, but it should do in a pinch."

"Okay. Take her there and stay with her."

"What about Hans?"

Mercer rubbed his eyes. He wasn't in any condition to go to the Bauer residence. Hans was already chomping at the bit to get back in the field. Seeing Mercer in his current state of disarray would convince the younger man the team needed him, potentially setting back his rehab by months. "Change of plans. You stay with Hans. Bas will stay on top of the coppers, and I'll take Lucie to the safe house."

"If you insist, commander."

Mercer found Lucie, who appeared wilted and on the verge of a breakdown. He didn't enjoy dealing with others' emotional turmoil, particularly when he felt his own grip on sanity was slipping away the longer he remained in limbo, waiting to discover Vogel's fate. He took the keys Donovan handed him and sat on the sidewalk beside her.

"Argus asked that I find a place for you to stay until things are sorted," Mercer said. "Is that okay with you?"

"Yeah."

He stood and held out a hand to help her up. She took it, and he led her to Donovan's car. Even though it should be safe, he checked for devices and trackers before climbing inside and starting the engine. After ensuring they weren't being followed, he drove to one of their rented flats and parked. It wasn't up to the team's usual mission standards, but this wasn't their typical mission. Hell, it wasn't a mission at all.

"You should change out of those wet clothes." He opened a closet, finding an assortment of items and handing her a clean shirt. "Are you injured?" Not bothering to wait for an answer, he went into the bathroom for medical supplies.

"I'm okay. Argus was shot. Twice." An overwhelming thought came to mind. "You saved his life, and I didn't even thank you." She looked teary.

"You should sleep. Food's in the kitchen, if you're hungry."

"Are you leaving?"

"No. I'll stay out here. I won't disturb you."

"You're hurt," she said.

He shrugged. The evening's events numbed him, which was unexpected. She gave him an uncertain look and disappeared into the bedroom. He waited for the door to close and silence to ensue. Then he let out the breath he was holding, feeling the bruises along his back and chest.

Returning to the bathroom, he examined his appearance in the mirror. His skin was streaked with blood and grime, a result of the explosion and the constant rain. It was a miracle he survived the building collapse. His skin stung from the dozens of cuts. Deciding a shower was in order, he turned the water to hot and stepped beneath the spray.

He braced his palms against the shower wall and let his head hang. He was knackered. He could fall asleep right here, but that wasn't wise. Turning off the water, he stepped out of the shower and dried off, rinsed his shirt in the sink, wrung it out, and hung it on the hook to dry.

He was seated at the kitchen table, picking tiny glass shards out of his shoulder when Lucie entered the room. She opened the fridge, finding nothing inside but a few bottles of water. She removed one and took a sip.

"I thought you said there was food."

"In the cupboards. Not much more than rations, really. Aren't you tired?"

"Tired. Wired. I'm not sure which way is up right now. I feel like I slept for a month, but it's been less than an hour. Talk about a power nap." In her overwhelmed state, she was rather talkative, much to his dismay. She unwrapped a protein bar and took a bite, making a face. "How do you eat this shit?"

"Sometimes, it's necessary."

"No wonder you're always in such a foul mood." Her eyes raked over his naked torso, observing the scars. She swallowed another bite, sighed, and put her snack on the counter. "Give me that." She crossed to him, taking the tweezer from his hand and sitting atop the kitchen table, directly in front of him.

Mercer made an effort to focus on her face and not her bare legs bracketed around him. She was in nothing but a t-shirt. She put her feet on the sides of his chair and twisted around on the table to dip a cotton ball in the rubbing alcohol before pressing it against one of the cuts on his neck. He hissed, and she pulled the swab away.

"You know, there are professionals who do this sort of thing." She pulled out a few flecks of glass from his neck and moved to the cut above his left eyebrow. "The medics outside my pub might have even done it for you. Scared of doctors?"

"I don't need a doctor. These are scratches."

"Is that what you call the rest of your scars?"

He didn't speak.

She finished removing the glass shards, put the tweezers down, and grabbed a tube of arnica from the first-aid kit. She squeezed some into her palms and put her hands against his chest. He stiffened, and she stopped and studied his face.

"It'll help with the bruises," she said.

"I can do it myself."

"Afraid I'm going to hurt you?" She flashed him a flirty smile. "For such a tough guy, you're being a baby."

He grabbed her wrists before she could continue. "That's enough."

"Bloody hell, Julian," she retorted with her usual level of sass, "you saved my life. You saved Argus's life and the lives of every single one of my customers. Let someone help you."

"I don't need help."

She tugged her wrists free. "Fine." She climbed off the table and washed her hands in the sink. "May I ask you something?"

"No."

She chuckled. "Too bad." She turned off the water and spun to face him. "The arsehole who destroyed my pub, is he the same man who murdered your wife?"

Mercer nodded, busying himself with the tube of gel.

"Is he dead?"

"That's yet to be determined."

"That explains a lot. Why I'm here. Why Argus is concerned with my safety. So, at the moment, this bastard is Schrodinger's bloody cat. He's alive and dead, and you don't have a fucking clue what to make of it."

Mercer glanced at her, wondering how she determined all that. "Perhaps."

"Well, I don't know what to make of it either, mate. But a few hours ago, I was almost shot to death. I watched the only family I have left get struck by two bloody bullets, and the only thing I can think about is how angry I am this shithead trashed my pub." She moved around him, watching the way he tensed the moment she drew near. Her fingertip ran along one of the scars on his back, and he jerked in response. "And you're still poised to strike, I see." She laughed. "Pretty ridiculous, isn't it? We're quite the pair."

"The pub can be repaired."

"Not everything can be fixed. Y'know, I never knew about Argus until my mum died. One day, he shows up, tells me he's my dad, says he's sorry, like that's supposed to fix things. He had a wife and a whole other family. When they found out about me, they left him. Honestly, Argus is a bit of a bastard. He betrayed them. He betrayed me and my mum, and he thinks showing up out of the blue one bloody afternoon would somehow fix everything. It didn't."

"Why didn't you toss him out?"

She crossed to her abandoned water bottle, picking at the edges of the label. "I did at first, but he wouldn't give up. One night, this guy wouldn't take no for an answer. Tried to rough me up. Argus saw what was happening, followed us upstairs, and beat the living shit out of him."

"The tosser filed a complaint."

Lucie's gaze shot up. "How did you know that?"

"Research."

"After that, I let Argus stick around. I thought he could fill the hole my mum's passing left in my life, but it didn't." Her eyes burned into Mercer's. "And tonight, I realized if something happens to him, I'll feel even more alone than I already do."

"Probably." Mercer had nothing encouraging to

say. He understood the emptiness she felt.

"You thought killing this tosser would fill the hole he created, but it didn't."

"No."

"Hate to break it to you, but nothing ever will." She snorted. "Aren't we a sorry lot? And there isn't even a bottle around to drown our sorrows." She watched as he capped the lid on the gel and placed the unused supplies inside the box. She waited a few moments before crossing back to the table and picking up the arnica.

Slowly, she massaged it into his back over the already prevalent purple and blue bruises. This time, he didn't fight her. After he relaxed into her touch, she planted soft, gentle kisses along his shoulders and neck. He let out a low growl, but it did nothing to deter her. Eventually, she slid onto his lap, her intentions obvious, and he carried her into the bedroom.

TWENTY-EIGHT

Mercer dropped her on the mattress and stepped away, zipping his fly and fastening the button. She moved toward him, letting out a harrumph, but his icy glare froze her in place.

"I thought you'd be more fun with your trousers off," Lucie quipped. "It's a big bed. You don't have to leave. We can share. I'll keep my hands to myself. Maybe."

"No," he said firmly. She wasn't thinking clearly, and even if a quick shag sounded pretty bloody fantastic, he couldn't let his guard down.

"We're stuck here for a time, aren't we? We should make the most of it. Have some fun."

He glared at her, solidifying his decision. His liaisons were normally straight to the point, without the need for exchanging names or making excuses. This was complicated, and it could get messy. He didn't want messy, nor did he have time for it. "This would be a mistake."

"Because of Argus?"

"No." The thought never even entered Mercer's mind, and even now, it seemed like a ridiculous notion.

"Then why?" She laid back against the pillow. "Did you take a vow of celibacy?"

"No."

"Then I don't see the problem." She rolled over. "I'm a fantastic shag, and you definitely have something pent-up you need to work out. Seems like we both can get what we want."

Mercer didn't bother replying before stepping out of the room and closing the door. He rubbed his eyes and settled onto the couch. "Birds."

Bastian's security measures were active and in place. It was unlikely Thomas Vogel posed any danger since it was doubtful he survived. It should be safe to sleep. But something felt off.

How did Vogel know they were meeting at the pub? When did he have time to set up on the rooftop? Why would he plant enough explosives to take down the entire building? Did he have an escape route? An evac plan? Vogel was far too fond of himself to commit suicide, and he was too well-trained and far too intelligent to make a mistake. Bastian mentioned Vogel might be working with an accomplice or a team. Perhaps one of Vogel's men turned against him.

Mercer struggled to get comfortable on the couch. This started as retribution for Michelle's murder, but if a team of psychopaths was running amok, no one was safe.

Closing his eyes and forcing his thoughts to quiet, he willed his body to sleep, but these questions wormed their way through his subconscious. He woke more agitated than when he fell asleep. Thankfully, Lucie's door remained closed, so he didn't have to deal with her.

Checking the time, he dialed Bastian. "Have they identified the remains yet?"

"Two of the bodies were members of the tactical unit. We haven't received any type of confirmation on the third one yet," Bastian said. "The military buried Vogel's records when he joined the SAS. It's why we didn't get a hit on the DNA at the scene of the park bombing. I'm not sure he's in the system or if the police have access to the military databases. Someone from MI5 is working on it. How are you holding up?"

"Last night left several unanswered questions. We need to discuss them further." Mercer went into the bathroom and pulled his shirt over his head, catching a glimpse of the dark, painful marks on his chest. No wonder it hurt to breathe. "Any progress on Bishop or identifying Vogel's other assets?"

"Inspector Brickle is assisting me on that endeavor."

"You can't trust him."

"We'll see, Jules." Bastian said something to someone else which Mercer didn't quite hear. "There's been a development. Let me ring you back."

While he waited for Bastian to phone, he stalked the tiny suite. Something nagged at him. His instincts told him this wasn't over yet. It couldn't be this easy. Everything was too simple, even Vogel's death. The problem was the limited visibility on the rooftop.

Mercer never caught a definitive glimpse of the person on the rooftop. He never positively identified Vogel. But he knew, without a doubt, the sniper fire came from Vogel. The shaped charge on the door and the tripwire on the rooftop were moves Vogel would make. Bringing down the entire building was an audacious move, similar to the failed attempt inside the furnace.

It fit the profile, but Vogel must have had a plan.

Perhaps his plan failed. Maybe the narcissist overestimated his own skills and perished at his own hand. That notion irked Mercer, but if that was the case, he would find some way to let it go. He wished he could go home or to the cemetery. He wanted to feel close to Michelle and tell her the news, even though he doubted she could hear it. He knew that desire was to satisfy his own selfish needs.

The phone rang, and he grabbed it, appreciative for an escape from his thoughts. "What?"

"The police received an anonymous tip about last night's explosion. With a little help from yours truly, they traced the number to a grocer's business line. It's another shop owned by the same grocer who rented Bishop the flat. That can't be a coincidence. The police are planning an invasion. DCI Yancy will be leading the charge. Shall I stick with him?" Bastian asked.

"Negative. Our priority is the identification."

"But Jules, if Vogel's working with someone or isn't dead, we need to take precautions."

"I know. Send me the address. I'll rendezvous with the police."

"At this rate, they might put you on the payroll. What about Lucie?"

"I'll take care of it." Mercer went down the hall and banged against her door. "Get dressed. We're leaving."

"What? Why?" she asked.

"Dressed. Now," he repeated.

She tugged on her clothes from the night before. "Did something happen? Is Argus okay?"

"He's fine. I have to leave, and you can't stay here alone."

"Afraid I'll clean the place out?"

"My team is spread thin. This will alleviate the issue. And where we're headed has a kitchen with a much better selection." Plus, Hans and Donovan would be on-site to handle any potential threats.

"You had me at breakfast." She grinned. "If you had played your cards right, you could have had me on the breakfast table."

He rolled his eyes, glad to drop her off at the Bauer residence.

*   *   *

"Nothing but bodies," Yancy said when Mercer joined him outside the market. The owner of the grocery store was dead, along with a few customers. "The upper level is empty. Literally, there is nothing up there. Camera was damaged. The video is wonky. Not sure any of it will be useful."

Mercer studied the exterior of the building. "I need to see inside."

"Have at it. And when you're through, we need you to come to the station to answer questions in regards to last night."

"You were there. You know what happened."

"Be that as it may, there are rules that need to be followed."

Mercer had no intention of assisting the police. Until recently, they never made any effort to assist him. All they ever did was muck things up, and even now, he wasn't positive their presence was anything more than a hindrance. Perhaps if he hadn't been concerned with protecting Yancy or the tactical unit from Vogel's sniper fire, the explosion wouldn't have happened, and he would be certain his wife's killer was dead. But based on this morning's carnage, it appeared the snake had slithered away again, and Mercer was stuck exploring a crime scene like some sort of investigator, hoping to find a clue as to where Vogel went, all while attempting to circumvent police procedures.

As Yancy said, the room above the market was empty. The only items inside were permanent fixtures. Mercer checked for surveillance devices and set to work, performing a grid search. He noticed a few scratches on the floor near the window. It could have been from a table leg or tripod. He checked the dust patterns, hoping to determine what had been removed, but the place was clean.

He went to the window and pulled the blinds, wondering if this position provided a vantage point. Something fluttered to the ground, and he knelt to pick it up. It was a surveillance photo taken of Mercer and Yancy from the previous evening. Written on the back were two words: *Your move.*

Mercer slammed his fist on the windowsill and dialed Bastian. "Vogel's alive."

"Are you sure?"

"Yes."

"So who's the bloke in the body bag?"

"Find out." Mercer shoved the phone into his pocket. Vogel came here after the explosion. He left the photo, eliminated witnesses, and made the call from the downstairs phone. How did he survive?

Scanning the entire room, Mercer opened the closets and built-in cabinets, searching inside for hidden documents or concealed compartments. Vogel chose this place for a reason. He knew Mercer would find it, which is why he left the photo and note. It was a taunt or threat. Vogel wanted Mercer to know the hunt was not over. He was giving Mercer a sporting chance.

When Mercer opened the coat closet, he found wooden hangers. Shoving them out of the way, he felt along the back wall. The police should have done as much, but they weren't familiar with tradecraft tactics. It didn't sound hollow, but Mercer spotted two drilled holes near the bottom. A nail was wedged in the corner of the closet, which Mercer used to slide the panel open. The false back was a solid piece which opened like the cover of a book. It had been pressed against the rear wall, making it appear to be one solid wall. Photos, blueprints, and notes were taped to the back of the fake wall, and four, tiny flat screen monitors broadcasting current surveillance feeds were attached to the actual wall.

The images sent an immediate chill through Mercer. His thoughts scattered. He had to move, but before he did, he had to be certain of Vogel's next target. One misstep would have lethal ramifications. Grabbing his phone, he dialed Bastian again.

"Pick up." Mercer impatiently waited for the analyst to answer.

"I may work miracles, but I'm not that fast."

"Be very careful what you say. Don't look around."

"Jules?"

Mercer watched the analyst gnaw on the end of a pen. "He's watching. He spliced into the security cams at police headquarters, or he planted his own."

"Okay. Where?"

"At your nine o'clock. He has three other monitors. One for the pub. Another outside the motel where we last met." The fourth was the most disconcerting. "And the last is positioned outside Hans' house."

"Are you certain they're live feeds?"

"You keep chewing like that and your lips are going to be black for a week."

Bastian dropped the pen. "Guess so, mate."

"Evacuate the building. Vogel enjoys killing coppers, and I doubt he wants us to get an identity for the dead man. He wants to fake his own death, and there's no better way than by destroying evidence to the contrary. He might have the building rigged or is planning a strike."

"I'm on it." Dropping the pen beneath the desk, Bastian bent over to pick it up. "I suspect he planted his own camera. I'll find a way to loop the feed, and we'll clear out before he's the wiser."

"Make sure the police maintain radio silence. We can't risk Vogel being tipped off." The thought of someone on the inside working for Vogel crashed through Mercer's forethoughts, but he couldn't control that. "Once you're clear, rendezvous with the rest of the team."

"Godspeed," Bastian said, disconnecting.

Mercer turned his attention to the last monitor, raced out of the flat, and down the steps. He burst through the market's front door and dashed to his car. Yancy called out to him, but Mercer didn't slow. Vogel was preparing to kill again.

TWENTY-NINE

Mercer didn't waste any time. He drove at breakneck speed to the Bauers' home. Along the way, he dialed Donovan and Hans. Neither answered, and Mercer feared the worst. Even injured, Hans was a formidable opponent. Attempting a strike against two former SAS operatives wouldn't be easy. Vogel must be daft. But Mercer couldn't help but think this was precisely the type of maneuver Vogel would try. It was a challenge, and with two easy targets, Perdita and Lucie, inside, Vogel might just get the upper hand.

The car skidded to a stop half a kilometer from the house. Mercer didn't want to get too close. He didn't want to tip off Vogel if the psycho was already inside. He dug through the boot and removed a duffel bag which contained several weapons, a flak jacket, and binoculars.

After slipping out of his jacket, Mercer put on the tactical vest and loaded his pockets with the necessary tools of his trade: a dagger, two smoke grenades, several extra magazines, and a canister of tear gas. He put his jacket back on, placed a second handgun at the small of his back and made certain a round was chambered in his holstered weapon.

If a breach was necessary, he'd have to use nonlethal methods. He couldn't risk endangering the hostages. But he didn't even know if Vogel was inside. However, since communication with his teammates had been severed, he assumed the worst.

He closed the boot and climbed behind the wheel. He didn't want to draw any attention to himself. The last thing he wanted was for one of Perdita's neighbors to phone the bobbies. The police would muck things up, like they did last night, and he didn't want Vogel to rack up any more kills.

Peering through the binoculars, Mercer had no way of knowing what was going on inside the home. The blinds were closed, and the drapes were drawn. Those were precautions his team knew to take, but those measures made it impossible to see inside. Mercer thought about the blueprints and photos taped to the hidden panel. If Vogel had a plan, it wasn't spelled out.

"Maggie." Mercer couldn't recall the physical therapist's last name, but she arrived like clockwork. Hans would have been expecting her. Vogel must have known. He must have used that opportunity to gain entry.

Putting the car in gear, Mercer drove up to the house and parked horizontally in front of the drive. The house was situated almost twenty meters back from the street. It was a spacious country home Hans had bought for his mum after their first big payday. It was supposed to be in a safe neighborhood, where she could rest easy without worrying about unruly scoundrels breaking in. Obviously, he never counted on this.

Mercer stepped out of the vehicle, keeping it between him and the house, and reached for his phone. No signal. Vogel had activated a cell jammer. Radio communication might still be functional, but Vogel was smart. If he didn't block them, he'd be monitoring the frequencies for chatter.

Grabbing the binoculars, Mercer toggled through the settings, but he couldn't get a look inside. Vogel knew all the tricks, and he came prepared.

Despite his anxiety and overwhelming desire to storm inside, Mercer performed a careful check of his surroundings. The property wasn't conducive to a sniper's nest. He didn't see any booby-traps or overt surveillance equipment. However, Mercer located the hidden camera.

Watching the house for signs of movement, he went to the mailbox and plucked the sticky cam off the back of the wooden post, dropped it into a patch of grass, and crunched it beneath his boot. A moment later, the drape moved half an inch.

Taking cover behind the car, Mercer waited. A minute later, the front door opened, and Donovan stepped out. He didn't move more than two steps from the doorway.

"Jules," Donovan said, "he wants to negotiate."

"All right." Mercer's eyes darted from Donovan back to the doorway. "Is he alone?" Donovan didn't answer, but he blinked twice. "Is everyone unharmed?"

"Take the radio." Donovan tossed it halfway to Mercer. As if pulled by an invisible force, Donovan stepped back through the doorway. His eyes remained on Mercer until the door slammed.

Mercer moved the vehicle closer, parked in the grass, and stepped out. He picked up the radio and hunkered next to the front tire, waiting for Vogel to speak. At first, it was nothing but static interference. A moment later, the killer's voice resonated from the device.

"I said we weren't through negotiating. Before you try something heroic, you should know I have the windows wired with explosives. Do your best not to shake things up too much."

"What do you want?"

"Ah, that's more like it." Vogel let out a maniacal laugh. "I remember when Michelle asked me the exact same thing. That was before the screaming and crying. I really thought she'd beg, but she didn't. It was disappointing."

Mercer dropped the radio, clasping the gun so tightly in his hands he almost snapped his own fingers. He couldn't see or breathe. His heart raced, the adrenaline pumping, and his muscles tightening. He was overcome with the desire to kill this sick, twisted piece of shit.

"I'd like to hear you beg," Vogel said.

"Please," Mercer managed through clenched teeth, "let them go. This is between us."

"No, it isn't. Your team would do anything for you. They'd die for you. If you don't do precisely what I say, they'll get their wish."

Mercer scanned the area. Vogel said the windows were rigged, but that could be a lie. He didn't mention the back door, and since Donovan went out the front, there was one obvious route in and out that wasn't wired. "Tell me your demands."

"You have to earn my trust, Julian. I have to believe you, and I don't. So your job is to change that. I know how this game is played. The moment you try to trick me, I will kill someone you care about."

"You will pay for the things you've done."

"Talk, talk, talk. I'm growing bored of the idle

threats. Make a move, or play by my rules. The choice is yours."

Mercer remained silent. His body still, like a cobra poised to strike.

"I'm taking your silence as acquiescence to my terms. The first thing I want you to do is come out from behind the car."

"Like I'm that bloody stupid."

"Remember, I'm the one in charge. You are fulfilling my demands. Not the other way around." Vogel waited five seconds, but Mercer didn't budge. "Come out, or I'll put a permanent smile on Hans' mum." Even at this distance, Mercer heard the scream from inside. "You have five seconds to comply."

Mercer took a few steps away from the car, holding the radio in one hand and aiming his gun at the house with the other. "I did what you said."

"Do it faster next time."

Another scream sounded from within.

"If you harm the hostages, I will no longer cooperate. That's a necessary condition for any negotiation. You called it trust. If I can't trust you, this ends now." Mercer could barely hear over his own pounding heartbeat.

"These aren't normal hostages. The same rules do not apply."

"Yes, they do. You have weapons. You made threats. This is no different. I need proof of life."

"My god, do you hear yourself? You're nothing but a brainwashed tosser. Still doing their bidding. Still following rules and living by some bloody code of conduct. When are you going to wake up? Your wife is dead, and what did they do about it? Nothing. What thanks did they show you for your sacrifice? Nada. They left you alone, disgraced, with nothing."

Not nothing, Mercer thought, *the burning desire*

for revenge. He gripped the radio tighter, knowing he had to keep the bastard talking, even though each second crushed his soul. With any luck, Donovan and Hans would come up with a plan, and they would end this. "Who are *they*? Is that what they did to you?"

"After my troop was held hostage, we were damaged goods. We were stuck stateside, working recoveries and hostage scenarios. We weren't fit to be placed overseas. They treated us like a waste of space, second-class citizens, nothing more than worthless, expendable foot soldiers. They wished we died in that camp. We used to be the elite. The most elite. And now, we were sent to respond to domestic terrorism and save diplomats from abductions. MI5 could handle it. Fuck, what am I saying? Those wankers formed a task force with New Scotland Yard, and even with the bobbies help, they still couldn't solve a string of murders."

"You're better than they are," Mercer said, the words sour on his tongue.

"Yes, I am. And it's about time they realize it. Last night was just a taste of things to come."

"No," Donovan's yell sounded over the radio, followed by gunfire.

Mercer moved quickly toward the house.

The radio chirped again. "Back away, Julian."

"Proof of life," Mercer demanded.

The front door suddenly opened, and Mercer shifted his aim. Vogel remained out of sight, but the barrel of a rifle was pointed at Donovan's head.

"Back away, commander." Donovan's eyes remained fixed on Vogel.

"Is everyone alive?"

Donovan nodded. "For now."

"Back up," Vogel bellowed, and Mercer took a step back. He kept his aim on the edge of the doorframe. If

Vogel came into view, Mercer would risk taking the shot.

"Okay." Mercer walked backward toward the car. "Take it easy."

"Call Bastian," Donovan said, his words rushed and urgent. The butt of the rifle connected with his face, causing him to sag. "He just detonated another bomb." Before Donovan could say anything else, the door slammed shut.

THIRTY

Mercer hunkered behind the car. Bastian was told to evacuate police headquarters, but there was no telling if that was the site of the latest detonation. The cell jammer made it impossible to phone out. Mercer tried hailing Vogel over the radio, but the killer was no longer in a talkative mood.

The negotiation was a charade. Vogel had no intention of allowing any of the hostages to live. He only wanted to torment them. Perhaps he realized it was the only way to delay his own death. The woman he grabbed from the gardens was a gamble. Vogel couldn't be certain Mercer wouldn't kill her and chalk it up to collateral damage in order to hit his target, so he took the people Mercer cared about the most—his team. Keeping them captive would keep him alive that much longer.

That knowledge flipped a switch inside Mercer's brain. Vogel wanted to be in the power position, but Mercer didn't have anything the killer wanted. In actuality, the killer had something Mercer craved more than life itself. His own safety and existence were meaningless tools, only necessary until Vogel was extinguished. Mercer didn't have to survive the ordeal. He just had to survive long enough to save his team and put an end to Vogel.

A one-man breach was out of the question. Mercer would have to find another feasible option. He'd have to lure Vogel out. But first, he needed to call Bastian. Donovan risked his life to get that message out, which meant it was important.

After studying the house and vantage points, Mercer edged to the rear of the car. If he stayed low to the ground, he should be able to make it to the street before Vogel spotted him. From there, Mercer could make a run to the nearest cover position, which would be the neighbor's skip.

Mercer kept the radio close. If Vogel had the audacity to speak again, he would be in for an unpleasant surprise.

Mercer scurried to the skip and ducked behind it. He placed the radio on the ground and removed the phone from his pocket. Surprisingly, he had a signal.

"Donovan said to call," Mercer said.

"Is he with you?"

"No. Vogel has him. Lucie and Perdita as well. Hans must be in there and possibly the physical therapist, but I can't be sure. Vogel attempted another detonation."

"Guess the chaps in bomb disposal handled it. We just completed the evac of HQ. I'm on my way to you. The police are sending units."

"They need to stay away."

"I'll do what I can," Bastian promised.

Mercer returned to the car and tried the radio again. "Fuck it." He darted to the side of the house and pressed his back against the brick. He peeked around, checking the front. Then he moved to the rear.

Perdita had a decent sized backyard where she gardened. Only a smattering of shade trees littered the area. They weren't large enough to provide cover. The trunks were barely larger than Mercer's thigh. On the bright side, Vogel wouldn't be able to use them for much of anything either.

The back door led directly into the kitchen. Mercer knew the layout of the house from his previous visits, but he had to assume it was wired. Edging to the right of the rear exit, Mercer hoped to see inside, but the small window was papered over. As gently as possible, he tested the handle, curious if the door was locked. It didn't budge, so he swiveled to the other side of the door and continued around the house.

All the back windows were shut tight and blacked out. When he came to the other side of the house, he located the power box. After a quick look around, he flipped the switch. The system let out a moan before shutting down. A moment later, the radio chirped.

"Fix it," Vogel snarled.

"Do it yourself." Mercer pressed his back against the wall and waited. There were no windows on this side of the house. If Vogel made an approach, he could come from either the front or back.

"Tut, tut, Julian. That is no way to speak to the man in charge."

Mercer pressed the radio, a sneer curling his lips. "You're no man. You're a rabid animal, and I will put you down."

"Not before I kill every single person in this house. Now turn on the bloody lights."

Mercer turned off the radio and returned to his previous position behind the car. While keeping one eye on the house, he rummaged in his bag for the binoculars. With the power off, the temperature inside would decrease, giving him a clear picture of Vogel's location. He just had to wait.

With the radio off, Mercer had no way of knowing if Vogel wanted to talk, but it had to be this way. This was a no-win situation.

A few shots rang out. Mercer pressed his lips together, resisting the urge to bark orders into the radio for Vogel to cease. The gunfire was an act of desperation designed to get Mercer's attention and force him to turn the power back on, but he wouldn't give in. This was his best chance of finding a way inside and saving his friends. But if it took too long, the killer would start tossing bodies out.

The moments stretched on for an eternity. Neither party willing to give in. Mercer looked at his watch, checked the progress the thermals were making, and studied the windows for signs of life. An SUV came to a stop at the end of the drive, and Mercer aimed at the intruder.

"It's only me." Bastian kept low as he made his way to the commander's position.

Mercer updated him on the situation. "We don't know the status of the hostages."

"They aren't hostages. They're our mates. And Hans' mum."

"And Lucie." Mercer regretted bringing her here. He should have left her at the safe house.

"What are his demands?"

"He doesn't have any. This is a showdown." Mercer thought about every previous encounter he had with Vogel. Each time, the killer dragged innocents into the fray as a means of escape. He turned the radio back on, but Bastian ripped it out of his hand.

"Detached indifference, mate."

Mercer's eyes flamed. Before this even began, it was personal. "He killed Michelle. Now he's going to kill Hans and Donovan. Don't act like you're detached."

"Vogel's good, but he can't hold his own in close quarters with Donovan and Hans. He must have them separated. He's using the women to keep them in line and make sure they cooperate."

"Or he's not alone."

"Let's see if I can get him to talk to me." Bas pressed the button. "Thomas, it's Bastian. Tell me what's going on."

"Turn the power on, or I'll kill someone else."

Bastian remained stoic, the way Mercer usually handled negotiations, but that was beyond the commander's capabilities at the present. Frankly, it was a miracle Mercer didn't storm through the front door. "I would, but Jules destroyed the entire box. It'll have to be rewired, probably have to get a professional to do it."

"Where is Mercer?"

Bas glanced at Julian, silently telling him to remain silent. "Your conversation wasn't productive, so I will be handling the negotiation from here."

"That is not acceptable."

Bastian dropped the radio to the ground and checked his gear. "Not a very talkative fellow, is he?"

"He talks too much," Mercer said. "We have to get inside. The longer we wait, the less chance anyone will survive."

"I agree, but we need a team."

"Our team's inside."

"Then we best get them out."

THIRTY-ONE

"You realize this is suicide," Bastian said, his voice in Mercer's ear. The pair were on comms. Mercer was at the front door, and Bastian at the back. It had been over an hour since the last attempted communication. "He must be feeling the pressure. He has to know we're planning a strike."

"I don't give a shit what he knows." Mercer was the decoy. The obvious target. He was the center of Vogel's attention, so he would breach from the front. Hopefully, it would cause enough of a distraction for Bastian to slip inside and get everyone else clear. "Let me know when I should knock."

"Just a minute." Bastian slid the fiber optic cable into the crack beneath the door, watching the screen as he twisted it from side to side to check for traps. "The back door is wired. It looks like C4."

"Probably a repeat from last night. He said the windows were rigged too."

"Like we're going to take him at his word." Bastian withdrew the cable and glanced around. Hans' bedroom was in the back corner. It was isolated with only one entry point. If the room was empty, it would be a good place to breach. "I'm looking for another way in."

"Make it quick."

Bastian inched the bedroom window up a few millimeters, just high enough to slip the cable inside. From this angle, he didn't spot any tripwires or det cord, but he couldn't be certain. Two people were huddled in the corner, bound and gagged. The bedroom door was open, but Bastian couldn't see any movement in the hallway.

"I'm going to attempt entry. Be ready on my mark. If it blows, shoot the bastard."

"Affirmative." Mercer crouched next to the front door, keeping his back to the wall to limit the chances of being seen from the window. If he wasn't concerned about triggering an explosion, he would launch himself through the window instead of attempting to knock down the door.

He took several deep breaths, calming himself before battle. He kept a firm hold on his gun, envisioning his next steps. Locate the target. Two to the chest. One to the head. No mistakes. It would be quick. It had to be. People he cared about were in jeopardy.

Flashing lights drew his attention, and Mercer watched in horror as DCI Yancy parked behind Bastian's vehicle. Mercer silently swore. "Abort."

Bastian held his position, watching as a shadow moved past the doorway. "SitRep."

"Yancy's here." Mercer heard footsteps and bolted off the porch, grabbed Yancy, and forced the detective into cover. "Hold your position. We have movement."

"What's going on?" Yancy asked. "Fifteen minutes ago, someone phoned, claiming to be Vogel. He said he has Lucie. We tracked the number here, but it can't be true. You promised me she'd be safe."

"We're handling it," Mercer said.

"How did he find her?"

The question felt like a punch to the gut. "I brought her here. Two of my men are inside. They will do everything they can to protect her. But you're in the way. Leave now." Yancy didn't budge, and Mercer couldn't risk dragging the man back to his vehicle. "Vogel called you here for a reason. He must have a plan, and it won't be good. Stay here and stay down. Do not fall for his tricks."

The radio squawked, and Mercer reached for it.

"I thought I'd invite someone else to witness your failure," Vogel said. "I hope Mr. Yancy enjoys the show."

"Jules," Bastian said over comms, "he's busy in the front room. I'm going in."

"Didn't you want to keep this between us?" Mercer asked into the radio. "Those tossers at New Scotland Yard can't investigate their way out of a paper bag. Why invite them to watch your undoing?"

Yancy gave Mercer a stern look, but he ignored it. The security specialist was doing his best to keep Vogel distracted. *Stay here*, he mouthed to Yancy. Then he crossed to the porch and ducked beneath the window. The drape moved, and Mercer froze. "Bas, how's it coming?" he whispered.

"Perdita's clear. Hans is...I'll get him out." Bastian ducked back out the window. Mercer turned to the side, catching a glimpse of the three of them as they moved northeast away from the house, continuing on a path that cut through several backyards. When there was no longer a clear line of fire, Bastian returned to the comms. "Vogel's working alone. No sign of Donovan or Lucie. He must have them someplace else, probably in one of the front rooms."

"Understood." Mercer took a breath.

"Jules," Hans' voice erupted in Mercer's ear, "Vogel flooded the house with knockout gas. By the time we came to, he was already inside. He kept us separated. There was gunfire. Mum said she heard screaming."

Bastian took control of the comm. "Jules, we need to reassess."

"Get them clear, Bas." Mercer slipped around the side of the house. Since Bastian used the window to get in and out, Mercer could do the same. Vogel couldn't keep watch everywhere, and while his back was turned, he lost two hostages. Now it was time he lost two more.

Mercer pushed the window open and climbed inside, finding remnants of a disabled device on the floor. Smeared bloodstains and torn pieces of blood-soaked sheets were balled in the corner of the room. Vogel worked Hans over hard based on the way Bastian had to carry him away from the house. Mercer swallowed as those images mixed with his memories.

He crept to the open doorway and peered into the hall. It was clear, so he quickly checked the other rooms as he made his way to the foyer. Several bullet holes lined the wall. Were Donovan and Lucie still alive?

When he ran out of hallway, he stopped. A tripwire separated the hallway from the main rooms. Mercer carefully stepped over it and peered around the corner. Donovan was chained to the pipes underneath the kitchen sink. He spotted Mercer and signaled to let the commander know Vogel was in the next room. Mercer crept across the tile floor and took a spot on the ground beside him.

Mercer examined the makeshift bandage wrapped around Donovan's leg. "Does he still have the blade he stabbed you with?"

Donovan nodded. "Grenades and an assault rifle, too."

"That won't matter if I get to him first." Mercer picked the lock and freed his teammate. Donovan moved to stand, but Mercer put a hand on his shoulder. "Not until it's time to strike. I don't want you bleeding out. That's your femoral artery, mate. You start moving now, you'll be lucky to last six minutes."

Footsteps sounded from the other side of the wall. The shadow moved from left to right, and Mercer cautioned a glance into the foyer, which connected to the living room.

"Bas, I have Donovan. There's a hitch. We need a distraction."

"I'm on my way."

"Jules," Donovan interrupted, "we'll have to move quickly. Vogel rigged a collar and leash of sorts. He put a grenade around Lucie's neck hooked to a chain. He has it fastened to his wrist. We drop him, the pin gets pulled."

"How much room do we have to play with?"

"Maybe forty-five centimeters."

"That's not much." Killing Vogel would result in the bomber dropping to the floor, and unless Lucie went down with him, the grenade would be triggered. "We need to get the collar off."

"Or sever her leash." Donovan glanced into the foyer. "Get me a proper angle, and I can make the shot."

Nodding, Mercer handed Donovan his back-up. "You better not miss."

"I won't."

Mercer slipped beneath Donovan's arm and helped him to his feet. As they moved to the next cover position, Mercer realized the drape was open and Lucie was pressed against the window pane.

"Lucie," Yancy screamed.

The woman shook with fear. Her stifled sobs indicated her terror. Donovan slid to a position on the opposite wall while Mercer searched for Vogel.

Vogel pressed the radio to his lips. "Julian, are you paying attention? If you don't show yourself, the lady might lose her head." He peered out the opened slats, hoping to spot Mercer outside. "I'm losing my patience."

"Vogel's behind cover." Donovan studied the pull on the chain. It was already stretched to its limit.

"Take the shot," Mercer ordered, moving through the kitchen to the opening on the other side which led to the dining room, which connected to the living room.

The floorboard creaked beneath his feet, and he ducked behind the wall. Mercer couldn't take out Vogel until Donovan freed Lucie. But he had the killer in his sights. He knew where he was standing. As soon as he heard the gunshot, he'd fire one of his own.

Donovan fired. The bullet tore through the metal links, severing Vogel's control of Lucie. At almost the same moment, Vogel fired out the window, shattering the glass. Mercer spun out of cover, but the killer was gone.

"Donovan?" Mercer bellowed, racing into the living room.

"I've got her. Get him."

Mercer dove out the window after the killer.

Yancy was engaged in a firefight with the killer. The detective fired, striking Vogel twice in the chest, but it didn't even slow him down. Vogel returned fire, and Yancy went down.

Mercer aimed for Vogel's head, but the killer ran in

a zigzag, ducking and weaving. Needing a larger target, Mercer shot him in the leg, sending him sprawling.

Vogel twisted on the ground, spraying bullets toward the house. Mercer rolled to the side, getting behind the car. Yancy remained prone on the grass. Unlike last night, Vogel didn't miss. The bullet struck Yancy in the chest, but Mercer didn't have time to stop. He kept moving.

"You're done." The spray of bullets ceased, and Mercer vaulted over the boot of the car. "Stand and fight."

Vogel was no longer on the ground. He got back on his feet and jumped into the police car. As Mercer raced toward him, Vogel gunned the engine. Mercer emptied the rest of his gun into the vehicle, puncturing one of the tires and putting several holes through the back window and into the boot. Unfortunately, even that didn't slow Vogel down.

Mercer threw himself into the nearest parked car and raced after the killer. "Bas, Yancy's down. Donovan needs medical assistance. Lucie's condition is unknown."

"Jules, where are you?"

"In pursuit."

THIRTY-TWO

Mercer had tunnel vision. His sole focus was Vogel. The killer would not get away again. He stomped harder on the accelerator. He had no idea where Vogel was going, but the killer was doing his best to lose the tail.

A piece of rubber tore loose from the damaged tire, and Vogel veered hard to the right to correct for the sudden shift. The tire rim shot sparks into the air as it spun against the asphalt. Mercer angled his vehicle and slammed into the corner panel of the police cruiser. Since Vogel's car was already off-balance and given the velocity at which it was traveling, it spun several times before screeching to a halt.

Mercer jumped out of the car. He dragged Vogel from behind the wheel and threw him to the ground, kicking him hard in the stomach, then the groin, and finally the back when the man rolled over.

"You killed my wife." Mercer grabbed Vogel by the shoulders and slammed him against the ground. "Why? Why Michelle? Why me?"

Vogel rolled and pushed against Mercer's chin, trying to force the commander off him. "We're the same," Vogel eked out, elbowing Mercer across the cheek. "We kill. It's all we know."

"The enemy, not innocents, you fucking psycho." Mercer drove his knee into one of Vogel's gunshot wounds.

"They made us, mate." Vogel jabbed his thumb into Mercer's eye. "They want us untethered. It makes us better weapons. I made you unstoppable."

All Mercer saw was red. It was true. He was nothing now but a weapon. And his job was to destroy the man who took everything from him. He lost all sense of time and awareness. He was blinded by his need for vengeance. As he struck Vogel over and over, he couldn't see or feel or hear. Higher brain functions were off. He was acting on autopilot, fulfilling only the basest of desires, giving in to the years of torment that wracked his every waking moment. This was payback for the injustices, the deaths, the bombings, and the hurt.

When Mercer surfaced from the rage blackout, he could barely lift his arms. His synapses misfired. He saw the condition of his fists and what little remained of Vogel's face. Muscle memory took over. He felt for a pulse, but Vogel was dead.

Mercer stood, his legs wobbly. Something wasn't right. He couldn't pinpoint what it was. He scanned the street for something familiar, but everything was strange. He was unsure where he was or how he got here. Everything was a blur. The light suddenly dim. His only desire was to return home.

Getting behind the wheel, he drove out of the neighborhood, unsure which direction he was heading. The compass on the rearview mirror indicated he was moving west. Somehow, he ended up on a familiar path. He felt himself drifting, the car lurching over the line, but he corrected, blinking several times to try to focus.

He saw the house and stopped the car, abandoning it in the middle of the street. He fumbled to get the key out of his pocket, wondering where all the blood came from. As soon as he stepped inside, he went into the kitchen and collapsed on the floor.

"He's dead. Everything's going to be okay now, darling. He's gone. He can't hurt you." Mercer stared at the ceiling. He could feel her. She was so close. He stretched out his hand, as if to reach for her. He was seeing her from that afternoon. "You're okay. You're okay." He rolled onto his side, curling in on himself, and wept. His body gave out, and he sunk into the abyss.

Minutes later, the front door slammed. "Jules?" Bastian's worried tone brought Mercer back to consciousness. The analyst was shaking him.

"Leave me be." Mercer shoved his friend's hand away.

Bastian knelt beside him. "Sorry, mate. I can't do that. Michelle wouldn't want this for you. She would want me to make sure you're all right. The police found Vogel's remains. They're scooping him off the pavement. Are you okay? I heard through the comms. I..."

"Help the team."

Bastian rolled Mercer onto his back. "Jesus." Vogel's blade was buried to the hilt in Mercer's side. Bas tore away Mercer's vest and shirt, finding five other stab wounds, all to the side where the vest fastened. Bastian dialed while searching for towels. Michelle always kept them in a drawer beside the sink. Thank god, no one ever finished packing up the house.

Mercer propped himself against the counter, watching Bastian scurry about, unaware why he was so frantic. "Vogel's dead. It's over. You can stop."

"Julian," Bastian's tone hit a nerve, and Mercer surfaced from the fog, "he will not take you too." Bas spoke into the receiver, requesting medics and giving the address. Hanging up, he attempted to staunch the bleeding.

"Donovan?"

"He'll be okay."

"Hans?"

Bastian pressed his lips together. "We'll talk about this later."

The fire ignited in Mercer's eyes. Some things still mattered. "Answer me."

"He's already been taken to the hospital. He'll live." Bastian gave Mercer a grim smile. "Lucie's okay. You and Donovan saved her."

Mercer remembered Yancy's lifeless body and shut his eyes. He didn't want to hear the fate of the bumbling detective. Instead, he sighed. He was so tired. He didn't want to destroy anything else. He didn't want to be like Vogel. He just wanted to be left in peace.

Bastian nudged him. "Jules?" He tried again. This time, Mercer felt a sharp pain in his side. He groaned, watching Bastian press the towels against his wounds and secure them with duct tape.

"Go away, Bas." The pain was getting worse, and Mercer was determined to shut it out of his mind, along with everything else. He wanted his last thoughts to be of Michelle.

"Don't you fucking do this. Do you hear me, commander? That's a bloody order."

Sirens wailed, fracturing the silence. Mercer's eyes fluttered. He completed his mission. He achieved what he set out to accomplish. Why wasn't that enough? He was lifted onto a gurney and rolled out of his house.

*   *   *

In the days that followed, Mercer was in and out of consciousness. The first meaningful time he awoke, he found Inspector Brickle in a chair beside the bed. Thankfully, the tube down his throat prevented having to answer the inspector's questions, but Mercer listened while the man updated him on the situation.

"Thomas Vogel's dead," Brickle said. "We're not entirely sure how that happened. Not to say it's a great loss. We spoke to Lucie, Yancy's daughter. She cleared a lot of things up for us." He eyed the bandages wrapped around Mercer's hands. "The military has taken over the investigation. The Met will not be investigating further."

Mercer stared at the inspector, communicating with only his eyes.

"I'll let you rest." Brickle stood. "You're one of the lucky ones."

Mercer turned his head away. He was far from lucky.

The next time he opened his eyes, Bastian was speaking to a nurse. Mercer coughed, his throat aching.

"Easy, mate," Bastian said, "you just had your lung resected. You don't want to aggravate it too much."

"Report." Mercer watched the nurse scurry away. "Brickle was here before."

"That was yesterday. Our involvement in this matter is being handled. I don't believe any of the bobbies were working with Vogel. He had sticky cams inside their offices. He was keeping tabs on their progress and yours remotely, but I'm not sure about our mates in MI5. I'll need more time to review their access and connections to Vogel."

"The unidentified body?" Mercer asked.

"Working on it."

"The team?" Mercer's eyelids were getting heavy.

"Recovering, just like you."

THIRTY-THREE

"You're getting released today," a chipper nurse said.

Mercer stared blankly at her, his expression entirely unreadable. He'd barely spoken in days. His team was broken, perhaps beyond repair. And for the first time, he didn't know or care if they continued on. What was the point? His eyes narrowed ever so slightly, and the overly cheerful woman frowned.

"Why the sour puss?"

He continued to stare, unspeaking, at her. Her bright smile evaporated from her face, and she went to the doorway. She opened her mouth, decided saying anything else was a waste of breath, and stormed out.

Bastian appeared a moment later. "At least you didn't make that one cry."

Mercer's gaze shifted, and he shut his eyes.

"Jules, we need to talk about what happened."

"I spoke to the police. If they want to arrest me, they can. I don't care."

Bastian pulled a pack of cigarettes from his pocket. He peeled open the cellophane and removed one from the box. He tapped it against Mercer's tray table, hoping to get a rise out of the commander. When Mercer continued to ignore him, Bastian removed a lighter and flicked it several times.

"Bas," Mercer mumbled, still not looking at him, "oxygen tanks. Go outside."

"You don't care if I pick up the filthy habit again?" Bastian challenged, a teasing quality to his tone.

Mercer's jaw twitched. "Pisser."

Bastian smiled, and the two fell into a comfortable silence until the discharge papers were brought and Mercer was declared fit to leave. "The team's in a state of disarray. Our flat is practically a boarding house, but we can make room for one more."

Mercer shook his head. "Take me home."

"Home it is."

*   *   *

Mercer sequestered himself in the bedroom he and Michelle had shared. Now that he fulfilled his promise, there was nothing left to do but mourn. The rage and hatred gave him energy and purpose. It masked some of the pain, and foolishly, he believed hunting and killing Vogel would bring him peace. But it didn't. It left him empty, his purpose stripped away. The void in his heart filled with sorrow.

He slept for days. When he wasn't asleep, he stared at her pillow. He replayed the conversations they shared and the hours they spent making love. He would never stop missing her. A part of him wanted to stay here forever. In a way, this was a new beginning, but he didn't want to start over. He was stubborn like that. He closed his eyes, tired and defeated. Right now, he couldn't fathom moving forward.

As had become the norm, he dreamt of her, reliving the pleasant moments. The grisly ending no longer haunted him, but the loss remained excruciating. Waking up meant losing her all over again.

She smiled, and he brushed the hair from her eyes. "You can't be serious," she said. "You'd never resign your commission."

"I could. What's to stop me?"

She straddled him, pressing her palms against his chest. "Me."

"You don't want me around?"

She brushed her lips against his. "You know the only thing I want is to have more time with you, Julian, but that's too selfish a thought to even contemplate."

"You can be selfish, my love. I'll give you anything you want. You just have to ask."

She let out a soft laugh. "The world needs you to do the things you do. I can't keep you all to myself." Her eyes grew more sincere. "When you're not here, I know it's because you're out there protecting me. I just wish this planet wasn't so screwed up, so you could be here more."

"Michelle," he protested, but she put her finger to his lips.

"Enough of this rubbish. I married you. I knew exactly what I was getting myself into. So you go save the world, and when you're done, I'll be right here."

"Promise?"

"Abso-bloody-lutely."

Mercer jerked awake, the dream a reminder of the conversation they had so many times. He flopped onto his back and stared at the ceiling. He'd been broken so long he wasn't sure there was enough of his heart or soul left to salvage.

He heard voices coming from beyond the door, so he climbed out of bed, stepped into the bathroom, and gave the beauty products on the counter a bittersweet smile. His reflection barely resembled the man in the photos on the nightstand. He was gaunt. His eyes black and sunken in. He had an unkempt beard from weeks of not shaving.

After a hot shower, one of the first in too long, he checked his stitches. The stab wounds were healing. He could almost breathe pain-free. He took out his shaving kit and tidied his appearance. He dressed in casual clothing, halting at the door when he heard Bastian's voice.

"We're not taking any jobs right now. The team's on the mend." Bastian paused. "I'll have Julian call when our status changes."

Mercer stepped out of his bedroom, finding Bas sitting stiffly in the living room. Cynthia was at his feet.

Upon seeing Mercer, the dog let out a happy bark and bounded toward him. Sensing something wasn't right, she wagged her tail and followed him to the couch. When he took a seat, she jumped up and licked his face.

"Why is there a dog in my house?"

Bastian smiled. "She has a name. Although Hans has been calling her Lucky. Poor pup thinks she's in witness relocation with the amount of moving about she's had to do lately, and with the cheeky sod calling her by a new name, I had no choice but to bring her here to get some peace and quiet." Bastian reached over and scratched her ears.

"That doesn't explain why she's in my house."

"Lucie's allergic, and since she's caring for Yancy until he recovers and her flat is out of the question, the DCI hoped we would do him a favor."

Mercer gave the dog a stern look, but she wagged her tail and nudged him with her nose until he moved his arm so she could put her head on his leg.

"The bitch has you trained, I see." Bastian rubbed a hand against his own chin. "Nice to see you aren't planning on becoming a lumberjack."

Mercer's focus went to the phone. "Was that about a job?"

"Are we talking about this now?"

"Yes." Mercer sighed. "Where are we?"

"Donovan's good to go. His stitches were removed two days ago. No lasting damage. He's waiting on your orders." Bastian went to the bar and poured a drink. "Hans' recovery has been set back a few weeks, give or take."

At the sound of hammering, Mercer peered into the kitchen. The room still brought about anxiety and turmoil but not to the same extent it once did. But the sound was coming from beyond the kitchen door. "What the bloody hell is that?"

Bastian hesitated, pouring a double scotch and handing it to Mercer. "I was getting to that."

Ignoring the offered glass, he strode into the kitchen. Cynthia followed, barking the closer they got to the door. He opened the door a crack and peered outside.

"It's good to see you up and about, mate." Hans wiped sweat from his brow. "Care to join? Maggie said it's good rehab, and it's pretty damn cathartic. Might make you feel better, unless you rip a stitch."

"Hans," Mercer said, relief flooding him, "are you all right?"

"Never better."

Mercer spun, a mix of confusion, annoyance, and relief on his face.

"Since Cynthia's going to be here a while, we thought it wouldn't hurt to put up a fence. The doctor said it would help with Hans' strength and dexterity as long as he doesn't overdo it. Donovan went to get more lumber. Thought we'd start here before we set to work on Perdita's house. Vogel caused a lot of damage. Nearly shot the whole damn place to shreds, but it would have been worse if we triggered one of his devices."

"I'm aware." Mercer leaned against the counter, feeling unsteady. Cynthia barked, pushing her head against his leg in an attempt to get outside. Distracted, he looked down at her. "You're a real pain in the arse."

Bastian found her leash and brought her outside, putting her on a lead so she could run about while the men worked on the fence. "Inspector Brickle handled most of the paperwork. We're lucky the police didn't expect more out of us, given everything that happened. But our mates at MI5 aren't as appreciative."

"Meaning?" Mercer asked, his gaze shifting to Donovan who was carrying several large pieces of wood into the backyard. "Should you be carrying so much weight, soldier?"

Donovan grinned. "Someone had to pick up the slack while your sorry arse was up in bed." He studied Mercer. "Are things back to normal now?"

"No. We have a dog."

"Speaking of, Donnie has a girlfriend," Hans teased.

"You're one to talk. How many physical therapy sessions can one man possibly need in a week? It's just an excuse to lure Maggie to our flat to shag," Donovan replied.

"Enough." Mercer turned to Bas. "What does MI5 want with us?"

"Since we had to call in several favors, they want to use us to solve one of their problems."

Mercer gave Hans a look. "How much longer on that shoulder?"

"Two months."

Mercer thought for a moment. "Does this have anything to do with the rest of Vogel's team?"

"They're all dead," Bastian said. "The remains from inside the collapsed building matched the man we know as William Bishop and the two *customers* found at the grocery store were IDed as the other members of Vogel's troop that were marked MIA. Apparently, they were working with Vogel, the extent of which remains unknown, but Vogel eliminated them."

"DCI Yancy thinks he was afraid they could be used against him if he was captured and not killed," Donovan said.

"And the leak inside the London police?" Mercer asked.

"Nothing conclusive. It looks like Vogel and his team took matters into their own hands," Bastian said. "Same goes for a possible leak at MI5." But something in the analyst's eyes told Mercer they shouldn't trust the policing agency.

"The last thing we need is to get caught up in someone else's mess." Mercer studied his teammates. "This last one was bleak. Things change. If any of you want to walk, you know where the door is. No hard feelings. You have family, friends, a dog. You can have a good life. You don't need this."

"Bloody hell," Hans exclaimed, "we're just getting started."

"No worries," Donovan assured, "this is precisely what we're meant to do."

Mercer looked at Bastian, knowing the analyst was committed to the team and their cause. Out of the lot, he was the most adamant about making reparations for their questionable acts.

"What about you, Jules? This is a nice place. You could get a Cynthia of your own and start a new career. The fish and chip place on the corner is hiring."

"That's not an option."

"Why not?" Bastian asked.

"Michelle wouldn't want that."

Bastian picked up the glass and toasted in Mercer's direction. "It's about bloody time you came to your senses."

Reparation

DON'T MISS THE NEXT INSTALLMENT IN
THE JULIAN MERCER SERIES. GRAB YOUR
COPY OF RETALIATION NOW.

ABOUT THE AUTHOR

G.K. Parks is the author of the Alexis Parker series. The first novel, *Likely Suspects,* tells the story of Alexis' first foray into the private sector.

G.K. Parks received a Bachelor of Arts in Political Science and History. After spending some time in law school, G.K. changed paths and earned a Master of Arts in Criminology/Criminal Justice. Now all that education is being put to use creating a fictional world based upon years of study and research.

You can find additional information on G.K. Parks and the Alexis Parker series by visiting our website at
www.alexisparkerseries.com